Vengeful Spirits

by

Jay Duckett

Bloomington, IN   Milton Keynes, UK
authorHOUSE

AuthorHouse™
1663 Liberty Drive, Suite 200
Bloomington, IN 47403
www.authorhouse.com
Phone: 1-800-839-8640

AuthorHouse™ UK Ltd.
500 Avebury Boulevard
Central Milton Keynes, MK9 2BE
www.authorhouse.co.uk
Phone: 08001974150

© 2006 Jay Duckett. All rights reserved.

No part of this book may be reproduced, stored in a retrieval system, or transmitted by any means without the written permission of the author.

First published by AuthorHouse 5/24/2006

ISBN: 1-4259-3449-8 (sc)

Library of Congress Control Number: 2006904207

Printed in the United States of America
Bloomington, Indiana

This book is printed on acid-free paper.

Dedication

To my late uncle, Jimmy Duckett. Jimmy passed away on December 31, 2005, after eleven long months of battling brain cancer. I love you, Jimmy. You'll always be missed and never forgotten. (Jimmy makes a brief appearance at Gaston's Oxygen Supply in the book.)

Acknowledgements

I'd like to thank Richard Crowder for his Civil War history knowledge and direction. I especially want to thank Natalie Braafhart for her support, encouragement, and months of hard work helping me type and edit this book. Thanks, Nat.

June 1865

Chapter One

Madison, Georgia

The humid summer heat in Georgia was bad enough on it's own but this year was made worse by the drought that its residents were painfully enduring. The ones suffering the most were the Confederate troops fighting in the War of Northern Aggression. Day in and day out these men fought for their way of life and their homeland in sweltering above 90 degree heat. During the day they sweat without relief, at night they lie in camp restless and hungry.

By now the Yankees were moving south on their campaign to take Atlanta. As they neared the southern city they burned and looted the towns along the way. Plantation owners were hanged, slaves were scattered, and families were ruined. Continuing to march south, General Sherman's troops entered the town of Madison re-supplying themselves by looting stores and homes along the way.

On the south side of Madison sat the Wells Plantation. It was a picturesque sight of the wealthy southern lifestyle. The estate was a modest two hundred acres. Scattered about the property were cotton fields, farmland, and a large pasture with livestock of all sorts. In each area there were slave quarters. By the cotton fields were the quarters of the labor slave Gregory Tate and the slaves that lived with him. Gregory, as the labor slave, was in charge of the slaves that worked outside and reported directly to the Master. By the livery stables there were quarters that held the slaves that worked with the livestock. By the large garden that supplied the fruits and vegetables for the plantation were yet another slave quarters that housed the men and women that worked the crops. In the house itself lived the house slaves Carl and Fannie-Mae.

The mansion and the grounds were easy on the eyes. The mansion sat at the edge of the southern tree line that separated the pasture from the cotton fields. Around the mansion was a well manicured lawn with large oak and magnolia trees providing ample shade from the relentless heat of the day.

The mansion was a two story masterpiece bathed in white with a wide porch that wrapped around both sides of the house. Four strong columns supported the roof

Vengeful Spirits

two floors up. In the center of the second floor at the front of the house was a large Widow's Walk flanked by two doors opening into the upper breezeway.

The interior of the mansion was spacious, clean, and tastefully decorated. There was a parlor, breezeway, library, smoking room, and a formal dining room on the first floor. A room for food preparation was at the rear of the house along with rooms for housing the house slaves. The cooking shed was a few steps behind the house. This is where the food was processed and cooked before being served in the dining room.

The proud masters of the mansion were Josiah and Miriam Wells. Josiah was a healthy 42 year old man of about 180 pounds; he stood 6 feet tall with sandy brown hair with streaks of gray. He was known by his slaves to have a good sense of humor. They had genuine respect for him, instead of the chronic fear of abuse that other slaves had of their masters.

Miriam Wells was a gentle woman, but not frail by any means. She could give as well as she got. She was stunning in her beauty even at her 44 years of age. She was proud of her husband for the man that he was. She wasn't the type of woman to fret about getting her hands and boots dirty doing whatever needed to be done. She had blonde hair, brown eyes, and a shapely figure that never failed to turn heads when she and Carl went to town to restock on supplies. There was pride in her stature, but it was not arrogant. She was a down to earth woman who did not take disrespect from anyone, yet she graciously gave respect when earned.

Miriam met Josiah in town at the dry goods store he owned. After seeing Josiah in the store several times and noticing that he went out of his way to help her, she found herself making excuses to travel from the north side of town, where she lived with her ailing parents. She would stop by the store or just ride by on her horse to catch a glimpse of him sweeping the boardwalk or talking with friends outside the storefront. Finally after several months, Josiah rallied his courage and asked if she would like to visit his home for lunch sometime soon. She accepted his invitation, they set a date, and after brief conversation Miriam returned home to tell her folks about her date, with excitement bubbling in her voice. She had remained calm while talking to Josiah. She didn't want to seem desperate by getting overexcited and frighten him off. During their first lunch together things clicked perfectly and within months Josiah had proposed to her. She accepted, and they were married at the Baptist church in town. Even after 15 years, she loved her husband more today than the day she married him in 1849.

Now that the war was practically in their front yard they regularly welcomed Confederate troops, on their way to the front lines, to camp in the pasture. While the troops were there Josiah would help care for the horses the men rode. He provided clothes and shoes when needed, and helped boost moral in the evenings by playing his banjo and singing along with the men that sat by crackling fires with pots of fresh stew, that Miriam had made, bubbling over the flames.

Miriam did her share of helping out, other than just cooking. A lot of the soldiers were, after all, only boys who were far away from home and with nobody to give parental advice; Miriam did the best she could. At times she would write letters home for the ones who didn't know how to read or write. Other times she would just sit and listen as these brave men, young and old, would talk of home and how things had changed since the war started. They hoped and prayed they would return to see their families again soon. At other times more practical matters needed attending to, such as washing clothes, preparing baths, or mending wounds. Sometimes she never got a chance to sit down, but through it all she always had a smile on her face, showing pride and respect for the soldiers she served. The Wells Plantation came to be known as the "Pasture of Grace" by the soldiers of the Confederacy.

Chapter Two

As the war drug on and the battle lines changed, the atmosphere on the plantation changed as well. There were always guard troops working in shifts while troops were camped out in the pasture. One night in the middle of June 1865, cannon fire from the guard posts roared to life. Quickly soldiers awoke and grabbed their rifles, loaded them, and took up battle lines facing the north tree line. A Federal scout party had been spotted at the edge of the woods at the north side of the pasture. For three days a skirmish took place and soon the "Pasture of Grace" had become nothing more than a killing field.

Within hours the Wells mansion had been turned into a field hospital. Men and women from town came to help with the casualties until Confederate surgeons could arrive to repair the wounded and to amputate the limbs of soldiers in order to save their lives. Many men died, some from extreme blood loss, many from infection, and still others died instantly as the crude ammunition tore through their bodies and destroyed vital organs on impact. The once quiet and pristine plantation was now a smoky, bloody, desert of death. The crops and pasture had been trampled to dust, and the stately plantation house was riddled with bullet holes and broken windows. The smell of gun powder, burning grass, and the rotting flesh of the dead soldiers cooking in the summer sun hung heavy in the air.

Miriam's heart was heavy for the boys who would never go home again. A tear rolled down her cheek as she surveyed the bodies of men whose wives would never hold them again. Seeing all of these men, who fought and died while being greatly outnumbered, fought to the death for what they believed in, made her proud to be a Confederate woman doing what she could for these poor souls of men.

After the surgeons arrived General Joe Johnston paid a visit to the famed "Pasture of Grace". Instead of being greeted by faithful men, he was greeted with the casualties of the Angel of Death. Dead bodies littered the pasture. The sounds of pain and agony wafted through the air. The smell of smoldering brush fires and rotting flesh filled his nostrils.

Vengeful Spirits

The General found Miriam and Josiah tending to the least wounded of his men. He gently laid a hand on Josiah's shoulder. "Might I speak with you for a moment?"

Miriam and Josiah stood together. Josiah said, with a surprised voice, "General?"

The General said, "I have some important issues to discuss with you. Is there someplace we can sit and talk?"

With worry on his face, Josiah replied, "Yes, I believe the parlor is empty." Miriam and Josiah led the General into the house, then into the now vacant parlor. Josiah motioned the General to sit on the cot under the window, while Miriam and Josiah sat on the cot opposite him.

Once everyone was seated General Johnston started by saying, "I cannot express my gratitude and my respect enough for the way you have taken care of my boys in their time of great need. Folks like you are the ones that make this fight possible." With a heavy sigh and a stroke of his beard he continued, "I have some bad news. I have received intelligence that reports the skirmish that took place here for the past three days was only an advance troop movement ahead of General Sherman. He should be here in two days. We can no longer defend the area due to the diminished number of troops and equipment. We will have to pull out no later than tomorrow night. I would suggest that you and the missus move temporarily to a safer location for your safety. I'm sorry." With a feeling of defeat, the General hung his head and stared at the scarred floor.

Josiah leaned forward, with his elbows on his knees, and said, "I appreciate your advanced warning, but there is nowhere for us to go. I guess we will stay here and hope for the best."

The General looked up at them in pity, then cleared his throat and said, "Both of you have done so much already, I am hesitant to ask anything else of you."

Miriam spoke up and said, "We are happy and proud to help in any way we can. What can we do for you General?"

With a grim look on his face, he said, "We have almost two hundred dead soldiers out there. We cannot possibly retreat with any speed with the load of that many dead men to carry. I would ask if you would donate a small portion of your pasture to bury my brave men where they fought." Miriam, and then the General, looked at Josiah.

With misty eyes and a smiling face Josiah stood and said with respect and pride, "General, I was proud to share my land with these men in life and battle; I would be honored to share it with them in peace and death."

With a smile of relief and gratitude, the General stood and shook Josiah's hand and said, "My men will take care of everything. Again, I cannot thank you enough for all you have done."

Josiah returned the handshake and said, "It was an honor, General." As the General walked out the door Josiah put his arm around his wife and asked, "We make a good team, don't we?"

Miriam laid her head on his chest, smiled, and said, "We sure do, sweetheart."

After supper Miriam and Josiah sat on their now beaten and tattered front porch, in their rocking chairs, watching the soldiers finish burying their dead. Lanterns bobbed and weaved in the darkness as low chatter could be heard. Out of the quiet of the night came the sound of a lone bugle. The slowness of the notes and the meaning behind them brought tears to both of their eyes. They could see through the faint light of the lanterns all of the soldiers standing with their hats off and their heads bowed. Some were standing with crutches, while others supported one another. Once the bugle dirge was over, the men quietly shuffled back toward their tents and recovery cots in the house.

The next afternoon, as the sun was sinking below the tree line in the west, the soldiers were slowly moving out. The hospital cots and equipment had been loaded onto wagons, and the dead had been buried the night before at the northern end of the pasture. The graves could be seen from the front porch of the mansion where Josiah and Miriam stood waving goodbye to the tired and war-torn soldiers on foot and horseback.

General Johnston trotted up on his mount and tipped his Stetson and said, "I will pray for y'alls safety and y'all will always be in my thoughts."

Josiah smiled and said, "Thank you. May the Lord be with you and your men." With a wave of his hand the General trotted ahead of the endless line of horses, wagons, and men retreating to the southern edge of the pasture.

The next day dawned with everyone working to repair and mend the plantation back together. Gregory and Josiah had gone into town and bought supplies. Windows needed to be replaced, barbed wire fencing needed to be strung, fence posts were replaced, and the household basics needed to be resupplied. Josiah didn't realize the amount of goods that were used to help the soldiers until they had to be replenished. While Josiah and Gregory were in town, Miriam, Carl, and Fannie were cleaning up inside. Most of the furniture and rugs had to be cleaned and put back in their place. The floors were peppered with dirt and grass, and the house needed to be aired out. The smell of medical supplies and blood still hung heavy in the air.

By sundown, the mansion and surrounding grounds were livable again. Tomorrow everyone would continue the long process that would return the plantation to its former splendor. The slaves had retired for the night and Josiah and Miriam again sat in the rocking chairs that occupied the front porch and enjoyed listening to the sounds of the night.

Suddenly, horses could be heard coming down the front drive. It sounded like troops slowly trotting. Thinking it was the last of the Confederate troops from town they remained seated. To their horror, it was General Sherman with a whole brigade of Federal troops behind him. Quickly both Josiah and Miriam stood up. They looked at each other with worry and fear in their eyes. They both knew that Federal troops might come through, but they thought it would be during the day, and not so soon, if at all.

As Sherman approached the house, with his troops in tow, Josiah and Miriam stood glued to the front steps of their once pristine mansion. They were afraid of what was going to happen. Knowing full well that the General's intelligence had told him that this land and mansion had been used for Confederate support and aid, they waited for the price they would have to pay for their allegiance to the Confederate Army.

Miriam and Josiah waited nervously as the General and his Officer dismounted their horses. Sherman stood and stared a moment stroking his beard. He turned to his Officer, spoke, and motioned toward the two on the porch. The Officer approached the couple holding hands and reached for Miriam's elbow. Miriam shrank away as if a serpent had been in his hand. He withdrew his hand and held it out, palm-up. Miriam looked at Josiah with doubt as she extended her trembling hand to the Officer. Josiah reluctantly let go of her hand as she was escorted down the stairs toward the famed and ruthless General. Josiah stood by himself anxiously watching from the front steps as Miriam spoke with the General who was known for hanging plantation owners and causing havoc no matter where he marched.

This was not the way he expected to eventually meet up with Union soldiers, especially not Sherman himself. Though the conversation seemed light, he could not hear what was being said. *Was the General telling her she would be raped, her husband killed, and her house burned to the ground?* The thought of this caused fear to grip his heart anew with icy fingers.

Instead of violence and pain hurled at the woman he loved, Miriam reached up and kissed the scruffy looking man on his bearded cheek. In shock, Josiah watched in disbelief as the destructive prone General gently took Miriam's hand and kissed it respectfully. Josiah stood with his mouth open and speechless as the Officer escorted Miriam back to the steps to join her confused husband. Once the two mounted their horses, the General looked at Josiah with a smile and tipped his Stetson.

With a commanding voice he yelled, "Move out," and slowly rode across the pasture and through the southern treeline with his troops, again in tow, until the sound of hoof stomps could no longer be heard, and they were gone.

Josiah turned to his wife. "What just happened? I thought we were going to be hanged for sure."

With a smile on her face and relief in her heart, Miriam responded, "Remember the story I told you about the boy I had an interest in when I was sixteen?"

Josiah thought a moment then answered, "You mean the son of your mother's friend?"

Blushing she said, "Yes, that's the one."

"Well….." Josiah said.

"Well," Miriam continued, "that boy grew up to be General Sherman."

Shocked, Josiah said, "I can't believe this. Our lives and our plantation were saved because you had an interest in him a lifetime ago?"

Miriam sat in the rocking chair on the front porch and thought for a minute. Finally she said, "No, I think it was because he also had an interest in me, but because daddy didn't like him and he knew it, he never approached the subject. I guess he always carried some sort of pleasant thought of me with him." With a reminiscent sigh, she finished by saying, "I guess this was the only thing he could do to show his respect and admiration for me after all these years."

Josiah sat a while, not saying anything, listening to the calming sounds of the night. With awe in his voice he finally said, "I must be the luckiest man south of the Mason/Dixon line. My wife had enough favor with the meanest General in the Union to spare both our lives and our home."

Miriam looked over to him and said with a smile playing around the edges of her mouth, "Apparently the General thought you to be a good enough man as well. If you remember, he gave you a friendly gesture of goodbye before he rode off."

The evening had gotten late at the once grand mansion. As Josiah stood up to stretch, before going in to retire, the house slave, Fannie Mae, opened the front door and announced that their beds had been turned down and she was retiring for the night.

Josiah turned to Fannie and said, "Thanks Fannie, we'll see you bright and early, we all still have lots of work to do tomorrow."

Jay Duckett

"Yes-suh, we shuh do," replied Fannie.

In an attempt at comedy, Josiah held out his hand to Miriam and said, "Miss, will you allow me to escort you to your room?"

As a warm blush covered her face Miriam played along and said, "Only if you will accompany me for the night." With a smile that should have cracked his face he responded by saying nothing. Instead he took her in his arms and kissed her moist, pouty lips with gentle touches of his own.

Chapter Three

In the early hours of the morning Josiah was awakened by the sound of running horses. He sleepily grabbed his pocket-watch. By the light of the full moon he could see that it was a little past three in the morning. It wasn't uncommon to hear horses walking across the fields at night due to the fact that the darkness provided good cover for Confederate troop movement, but these horses were running. Cautiously, he looked out the bedroom window to see eight Union soldiers on horseback approaching the mansion with their weapons drawn.

Without hesitation he shook Miriam and said, "There are Union troops outside coming toward the house. I wonder what they want."

"Maybe they have a message from General Sherman," mumbled Miriam, still half asleep.

With that, Josiah got out of bed and said, "Stay here. I'll go see what they want."

Halfway down the stairs Josiah heard loud banging on the front door. By the time he got to the door and opened it he was met with a pistol and a member of a group known as the "bummers". This renegade group of trouble-makers were A.W.O.L. Union soldiers. They had decided to no longer follow orders from the Union generals, but to wage war on their own terms, without having to answer to a higher authority.

As Josiah stood in the doorway in his underclothes, with a pistol pointed at him, the renegade soldier named Thomas Stringer said in a whisper, "Your plantation was mistakenly spared. We are here to rectify that mistake." With the threat having been issued, Stringer pistol whipped Josiah into unconsciousness and had him tied up and gagged.

The eight men quietly entered the house with Stringer in the lead. From upstairs Stringer heard Miriam call out to Josiah as the front door closed, "What did they want dear?"

Stringer told the other seven men to search the rest of the house for the house slaves and round up the slaves in their quarters and bring them to the house. "I'll take care of the missus," he said as he quickly strode up the stairs.

Miriam was just getting out of bed when Stringer stormed through the door blocking her escape route.

With terror in her voice she asked, "What do you want here?"

Stringer stared at Miriam in her nightclothes and said with a wicked smile on his face, "What ever I can get my hands on." Miriam jumped from the bed and made a move to the door, but even in the darkness of the room Stringer grabbed her by the arm and threw her to the floor.

Crying and screaming Miriam said, "Why are you doing this? General Sherman spared this house and our lives and said we would be safe."

Stringer said, as he was removing his boots and pants, "I don't answer to General Sherman or any other general. I answer only to myself."

The other seven men exited through the rear of the house by the food preparation room door. On their way out, they collected Carl from his room and took him to Fannie Mae's room, and both were bound and gagged. One man stayed with Carl and Fannie Mae, while the other six split up by twos and rousted the other slaves from their living quarters. From inside the house, the man guarding Carl and Fannie Mae could hear yelling and screaming as the slaves voiced their anger, fear, and hatred of the men invading their homes. As the yelling and screaming got closer a shot was heard and all was suddenly deathly silent.

A few minutes later Ken Jackson came into the room where Carl, Fannie Mae, and their guard were and said, "Oh hell, you're not gonna believe this!"

"What? What happened?" asked Eric Holden.

"We were rousting the niggers out of the shacks when out of nowhere this big guy tackled me to the ground and started laying into me." The man named Ken continued as he wiped sweat mixed with blood from his forehead, "Then the next thing was I heard a shot. All of the sudden I was being smothered by the weight of the big guy lying on me. I pushed the guy off of me and looked at him. The top of his head was gone! I looked over at James Carter holding a smoking shotgun. He smiled at me and said 'You owe me one'."

Eric looked at Ken, and then at his clothes and said, "So that's what all the blood is from. I thought you got shot."

Ken smiled "Nah, I didn't get shot. Other than the fact that I got blood and brains all over me, I'm okay."

Upstairs, Stringer had tried everything he could to rape Miriam. She was stronger than he had expected. Finally out of options, Stringer grabbed his pistol and put it to her head and said gritting his teeth, "I didn't want it to come to this, but if you don't spread those pretty thighs, things are going to get real messy." Stringer was straddling her at her knees. The thought of this smelly roughneck entering her made her nauseous. She stopped crying and with every bit of strength she had she brought her right knee up to connect with his crotch. It was a perfect hit.

Stringer dropped the gun, rolled over, and fell to the floor vomiting. At that moment the both of them heard a shot from the rear of the house. Miriam took advantage of the situation and jumped from the bed and bolted toward the door, stepping over Stringer in one leap. Though in pain, Stringer managed to grab Miriam by the ankle as she leaped over him. With a thud Miriam hit the floor hard, right on her face. Hitting the floor dazed her enough for Stringer to grab her other ankle and drag her back into the room. With her head pounding and her nose bleeding, she rolled over on her back.

She looked at Stringer standing over her and said, "Okay, I give up. Just get it over with."

Stringer was putting his pants and boots on and said, "It's not that easy, honey. You have really pissed me off. I'm past the point of giving you the pleasure. You will soon join your husband."

Once he was dressed, and his pistol back in his holster, Stringer pulled the sheets from the bed and ripped them into strips. Quickly he tied her wrists and ankles and left her sobbing and bleeding on the floor, wondering what had happed to her husband and what would happen to her.

Stringer hurried back down the stairs to find out what the shooting was about. He took the stairs two and three at a time, with his pistol in hand, ready to kill every last slave if they had gotten out of hand. Instead, what he found when he walked through the door of Fannie Mae's room was Eric Holden brutally beating and raping Fannie Mae on the bed. Stringer holstered his pistol and with an exasperated sigh he said, "I told you guys to get the slaves together, not get your jollies while there's gunfire outside."

Ken Jackson was standing inside the door with a repeating rifle pointed at Carl. In Eric's defense he said, "Awh, give the guy a break, James was the one that fired the shot." Stringer looked over at Ken. Even in the dim light of the lantern in the corner Stringer could see the blood and bits of flesh stuck to his vest.

"Then what the hell happened to you?" asked Stringer.

With excitement in his voice, Ken told Stringer the series of events as they happened. As he finished his story Ken added, "When I came in here to tell Eric what happened the fat woman started screaming and crying, "YOU KILLED GREGORY!" over and over again. Eric told her if she didn't shut up she would get what was coming to her, so….. I guess she's still getting it."

Stringer shook his head and said, "You guys are sick. Why would you want to ruin your pecker by sticking it in a nigger?"

Ken responded with a chuckle and said, "Hey, it's not that bad. I got me some from a real young-un when we were roustin' those niggers from the shacks. See, this girl wouldn't leave her bed so, I showed her what happens when she don't follow orders." Ken stopped then snapped his fingers. With revelation in his voice he said, "That nigger James shot must have been her father. That's why he jumped me."

"That would make sense," said Stringer. As Stringer took a last look at Eric he grunted, "Eeww! I still can't believe you guys." As he walked out of the room he said, "You two hurry it up, we got work to do. I'm going to check on the others."

As Stringer walked down the back steps and across the lawn he saw Gregory, just like Ken had said, lying on his back with the top of his head missing. His eyes were lifeless and staring into the night sky. A large pool of blood gathered on the ground under the gaping crevice where the top of his head had been. Stringer stood still and thought a moment then said, "Alright, we need to get these spades working."

He turned to James, who was still holding the shotgun level at the remaining slaves and said, "Take the women to the root cellar and lock the door. There are no windows down there so they can't get out. Be sure you lock the door when you leave."

James asked Stringer, "Why are we putting them in there?"

"The root cellar is just for safe keeping for now. We'll deal with them later," responded Stringer.

"If you say so, Tommy Boy." James sighed as he waved the shotgun at the women and moved them toward the root cellar. "By the way, where is the cellar door?" asked James.

Stringer pointed toward the house and said, "It's at the far end of the house in the back. You have to look to see it. It's hidden behind some bushes. I saw it earlier when I left the house." Stringer told one of the other men watching the slaves, "Go with him to make sure none of them try to run off." A young soldier trotted off to catch up with James.

The others were waiting for Stringer to speak. He stood thinking as he rubbed his dirty hands across his unshaven face. Eric and Ken came walking across the yard pushing Carl and Fannie ahead of them. Fannie started crying and wailing when she saw Gregory's body lying in a pool of blood.

Stringer said, "Oh shit, not again. Ken, take her up to the root cellar with the rest of the women. When you get to the back of the house, yell for James, he'll show you where it is. Then, the three of you come back here. Now move! We don't have much time left." Stringer said to the man closest to him, "Take one slave and go to the barn. Retrieve both wagons with what's left of the sorry looking horses around here. Then bring them to the front of the house. When you are finished wait for the others, they'll be along soon."

The man strode over to a middle aged slave, with his rifle he nudged the black man to his feet, and said, "Let's go." Slowly the slave started walking toward the barn. The man said in a gruff voice, "Make one wrong move and you'll get what the other nigger got."

Stringer watched until both of them had disappeared into the barn.

Stringer told Eric that they were going to use the slaves to load the wagons up with as much stuff from the house as they could. Eric stated, "The man was pretty well off. There must be some pretty good stuff inside."

Stringer savoring the thought responded, "Yeah, I noticed that the liquor cabinet was full of whiskey and wine when I walked through earlier. I am sure there is some silver in the house as well."

Eric smiled, "Do you think the old guy had a safe?"

Stringer shrugged his shoulders and said, "I don't know, but we'll find out."

Stringer stepped over to Carl, who was sitting on the ground with his head down, and pushed him with his boot and said, "Hey, house nigger." Carl looked up but didn't look into his eyes. Stringer asked, "Did the Master have a safe?"

Carl slowly shook his head and answered, "I don't know, but if he did it would be in his office next to his bedroom. That's the only room, other than the bedroom, that I wasn't allowed to go into, suh."

With a devious smile Stringer looked at Eric and said, "Well, I guess we'll just have to check it out won't we?"

At that point James came walking up with Ken and the young soldier trailing behind. "Okay, what now?" James asked.

Stringer said, clearing his throat, "We need to be out of here by sunup and that gives us just a few hours to finish things up. Ken, you and the boys take the slaves up to the house and start loading anything of value into the wagons. Start with the first floor and call me when you finish."

"Where are you going?" asked Eric.

Stringer said, rubbing his hands together, "You and I are going safe hunting on the second floor."

As Stringer and Eric turned and headed toward the house, he shouted to James, "Let's move it, sunup is not far away."

Chapter Four

Stringer and Eric first searched the bedroom; it was less cluttered than the office. Miriam lay on the floor, her nose had quit bleeding but she still screamed curses at the two men violating her personal space. Eric pulled the pillowcase off one of the pillows and shoved it into her mouth.

"That will shut the bitch up." Eric said with a smile. They had tossed the bedroom and found nothing.

Out of breath Stringer said, "Shit, it's not here. Let's look in the office."

As Stringer turned to go out the door, he noticed on the floor by his foot was Josiah's gold pocket watch that had been knocked off the bedside table. He reached down, picked it up, opened it, and read the inscription which read, *"To my beloved husband, Love Miriam"*. He then closed the pocket watch and stuffed it into his pocket. Both men quickly moved to the office and with building frustration began breaking furniture and tearing framed pictures and diplomas off the wall.

Now that the entire room was destroyed including the desk and chairs, Eric shouted, "Damn it, there's nothing here. The nigger must have lied to us." Standing near the door Stringer wiped his brow with a rag as he removed his hat. He noticed on the far wall one picture still hanging.

Stringer pointed at the lone picture and said, "Did you forget one?" Eric stepped over the now splintered furniture and with the butt of his rifle he smashed the picture square in the center. Instead of punching a hole in the wall, as Eric had expected, he heard a loud "CLUNK".

Eric turned and looked at Stringer and said, "Holy shit, I think we just found the safe."

He pulled the shattered remains of the picture from the wall and it crashed to the floor. There was the safe. It really wasn't much of a safe. Actually it was more like a strongbox mounted in the wall with a single keyhole. Eric's excitement quickly died when he realized that they didn't have the key.

As if Stringer was reading his thoughts, he said, "I remember seeing a key in a drawer while I was tearing the desk apart." Like a flash both men were on the floor sifting through the rubble that was once an imported desk from China.

Within minutes Stringer yelled, "I got it." Quickly he stood up and stepped over to the safe. As his hands shook with excitement Stringer unlocked the door and swung it open. Both men stared in awe and disbelief as several stacks of paper Confederate bills stared back at them.

Eric said, "I'll go get something to put this in." In a heartbeat he was back with the other pillowcase. The two of them filled the pillowcase halfway up and Stringer slung the sack, heavy with bills, over his shoulder.

He heard from the first floor James yelling, "Hey Thomas, we're finished down here."

Eric looked at Stringer and asked, "Are we heading out now? It will be sunup in an hour."

Stringer looked passed Eric toward the bedroom and said, "Almost, we just have a few loose ends to tie up."

Stringer and Eric stopped by the master bedroom. Stringer looked in on Miriam. She was still in the same spot on the floor with the pillowcase in her mouth. As he closed the door behind him, Stringer said, over his shoulder to Miriam, "I'll be back in a minute to take care of you, sit tight."

Once Stringer and Eric were back downstairs Stringer loaded the sack of Confederate bills into one of the wagons. He managed to hide it under a silver serving tray monogrammed with *"M.W."* in the center. Once everything was secured in the wagons

Stringer turned to Eric and said, "Go down to the barn and bring back the two longest lengths of rope you can find and hurry." Stringer turned to the other men and told them to line the slaves up on the top step of the mansion. The men looked at each other with misunderstanding on their faces then looked back at Stringer without a word. Stringer calmly said, "I know it sounds strange, but just trust me." The men then turned, shrugged, and started about their strange task.

Stringer turned to face James and said, "Go around back and drag that nigger you shot into the dining room. Once you get him inside use any lamp oil you can find in the house and douse his body. We're going to use his body as kindling to burn the house when we leave." With a disgusted grunt of the duty assigned, James turned and disappeared around the side of the house. Eric was back with the rope. He came up huffing and puffing to Stringer and Ken.

"We're in luck." Eric said. "I found two long hemp ropes that are both in good shape." Eric looked at Stringer and carefully said, "We don't have enough rope to hang all these niggers. What do you have in mind?"

Stringer patted the young man on the back and said, "We only need two for this job." Stringer instructed Eric by saying, "Tie me two justice knots in both of these ropes."

Eric nodded and said, "Okay. You're the boss."

While Eric was tying the knots, James stuck his head through the front door and yelled, "You want me to light him up now?"

Stringer turned and said, "No. Not yet. We'll start him up when we leave."

Now that the knots were tied, Gregory was in the house, and the slaves were on the front steps there was only one thing left to do. Stringer gathered his men together and told them of his plans. When everybody understood what was going to happen Stringer took James and went into the house with James carrying the knotted ropes over his shoulder.

Inside the house Stringer picked up the groaning and bleeding body of Josiah and carried him over his shoulder and up to the second floor like a sack of flour. Once all three men were on the second floor Stringer dropped Josiah on the floor at the end of the hall in front of the doors that lead to the Widow's Walk.

The Walk was bordered by a sturdy wooden railing that was attached to both the front of the house and the Walk with bolts. Stringer opened the doors to the Walk and stepped out. He waved to the men below and shook the railing to see how sturdy it was. "Perfect", he mumbled to himself. He turned around and said to James, "Go to the last door on the right and bring the missus out here. I'll take the rope and get started."

James trotted down the hall. He could see it was almost sunup and he needed to hurry. He opened the door to the bedroom and stepped in. It looked like a tornado had hit the room. Clothes were everywhere, the bed was a mess, and the dresser drawers were on the floor along with the few pictures that once hung on the wall.

Under the bed linen, which was now on the floor, he saw a foot sticking out. As he grabbed the foot and started to pull, Miriam started kicking and screaming through the pillowcase still in her mouth. All the floors in the house were polished wood and smooth so instead of picking her up James just grabbed the strip of linen between her ankles and drug her to the Widow's Walk.

When James reached the Widow's Walk Stringer already had the ropes tied to the railing. James dropped Miriam's feet and walked over to Stringer and said, "These are white folks, don't we usually hang niggers?"

Stringer stopped what he was doing and put a hand on James' shoulder and said, "Yes, usually, but this is an unusual situation. First, these people, along with their nigger help, supplied, nursed, and personally supported the Confederates. Did you see the cemetery made at the north end of the pasture? Those are Confederate burial plots. These folks did a lot more than just give water to the soldiers. General Sherman, in a moment of stupid oversight, spared this place and these people. I personally don't agree with his decision. Secondly, that bitch tied up inside wouldn't give me any. Instead, she kneed me in the nuts."

James had to swallow a chuckle because he could tell that Stringer's frustration was getting the best of him. He didn't want to swing from a rope like Josiah and Miriam. "I see your point, Tom," said James.

"Well, let's get to it. It's almost dawn," said Stringer.

Josiah was the easiest to fit for the rope. While his whole body ached and his legs barely worked he stood on his own, not having enough strength to fight back he did nothing else. The only emotion he showed was a trail of tears trickling down his swollen and bruised face.

Miriam was something different. It took both men to subdue and rope her. Stringer pulled the pillowcase from her mouth and said, "Would you like to say one last word before you meet your Maker?"

With anger and fear tearing at her mind and soul she growled out, "You bastards are animals! You and your seed will loathe the day you ever set foot on this soil!"

"Okay. I've heard enough," said Stringer, as he shoved the pillowcase back into her mouth. Stringer looked at her and smiled. He bent down and said to her, "Since you have been so much trouble, you get to see your husband die first, before you die."

"NO! NO! NO!" Miriam screamed through the cloth in her mouth.

With a grand gesture Stringer grabbed Josiah by the ankles and tossed him over the rail. Miriam continued to scream as the slack rope instantly tightened as Josiah's feet disappeared over the railing. Stringer looked over the railing at Josiah hanging from the rope. "Shit!" Stringer swore. "He isn't dead." He was kicking like a fish on a fishing line.

The slaves either looked on in horror or wept like children. The man they had grown to admire and respect was now strangling at the end of a rope, and they could do nothing to help him.

Miriam could only see the rope and the faces of the horrified slaves. As reality sunk in Miriam suddenly went slack and quiet. Everything was gone. There was nothing left to live for.

With a heavy shove, James pushed Miriam over the railing and said, "Your turn honey." Miriam went over the railing head first. When the rope caught, her feet swung down and the force of the fall didn't break her neck instead, once the rope tightened, it pulled her head from her body. James and Stringer heard a "THUMP" on the floor of the front porch.

They both looked over the railing and saw the headless body of Miriam lying under the still swinging rope. Her head had rolled toward the house and had come to a stop in front of one of the rocking chairs. Her eyes were wide with terror and the pillowcase was still in her mouth.
James looked at Stringer and said, "Damn! That wasn't supposed to happen was it?"
Stringer slapped James on the back and said, "You're better at this than I thought. Good job, my boy." Laughing, both men headed downstairs.

On their way downstairs they heard a thunder of gunfire, then silence. Stringer stopped and said, "Good, now we can get out of here before more soldiers come through here and catch us."

When they got to the first floor Stringer stopped in the dining room and pulled out one of the cigars he had stolen from the humidor in the parlor. He stuck it in his mouth and reached for a match from his vest. He struck the match on the wall and lit the cigar, puffing blue smoke into the stagnant room. Once the cigar was lit he knelt down at the stiff body of Gregory, with the match in hand, and lit his shirt.

Slowly, a blue flame ignited on the clothing. The flames soon caught the torso of the body on fire. As Stringer stood up, he flicked the still burning match at the smoldering body and it landed on Gregory's bloated cheek. Stringer blew out a mouthful of smoke and said, "Let's go."

On the front porch, Miriam's headless body had left a large pool of blood from the stump where her head had been ripped off. On the steps, the rest of the slaves lay dead with gunshot wounds to the back of the head. The porch was littered with blood and flesh and bits of tissue from the execution of the men that had called this place home.

As Stringer and James walked out the front door they passed the swinging form of Josiah. They saw his hands and legs twitch.

"Son of a bitch," said James, "he's still alive."

Exasperated, Stringer sighed and said, "Damn it if it's not one thing it's another."

With that he wrapped his arms around Josiah's legs and pulled. With a loud "SNAP" Stringer let go of the dangling legs and announced, "Now, he's dead." James jumped over the bodies of the slaves and mounted his horse. Stringer followed but kicked his way through the tangled line of corpses.

As Stringer hopped on his horse he looked up at the sky and thought, *it looks like rain.* The dawn had broken and the sky was covered by lead colored clouds. The air was humid and no wind was blowing. "We need to hurry if we're gonna beat this rain." Stringer told his men, "There's an old quarry just south of Loganville that has shelter. We will hide the wagons there for a while. Okay, let's move," yelled Stringer.

Eric hesitated as the others began to ride off then yelled, "Hey Tom! What about the slaves in the root cellar?"

Stringer stopped his horse and thought a moment, as he looked at the sky. As he turned his horse around, he yelled to Eric, "Forget 'em. We don't have time. We gotta get outta here." Eric took one last look at the house and shrugged and trotted his horse to catch up to the others.

As the bummers quickly rode toward the south through the tree line, the rain began to fall as if even the skies were mourning the atrocities that had taken place the night before.

By late afternoon the rain had stopped. The clouds had blown away and bright sunlight bathed the front porch of the now deathly quiet mansion.

Chapter Five

A group of six Union soldiers that were on patrol slowly rode down the rutted, muddy drive of the stately plantation. As the Captain approached the house, he suddenly stopped and held up his hand for the others to do the same. He slid off his horse and walked back to his Lieutenant and said, "Isn't this the Wells Plantation?"

"Yeah, the Confederates call it the 'Pasture of Grace'," answered the Lieutenant, still sitting on his mount.

The Captain adjusted his Stetson and said, "Well, we've got a big problem then."

"What's our problem?" asked the Lieutenant.

The Captain blew out a stressful sigh and said, "The bummers we've been looking for came through here."

"How do you know?"

"I just know," the Captain said as he shook his head and looked at his boots. The Captain took a few steps away from his horse and shouted to the rear of the line of soldiers on horseback, "Private, front and center!"

Quickly young Private Moore trotted up and saluted, "Yes sir." The Captain told the Private to retrieve General Sherman and tell him the bummers we've been tracking have plundered the Wells Plantation and murdered Mr. and Mrs. Wells.
"Now go quickly, we need him here now."
"Yes sir," the Private responded, and with the speed of the wind, he was gone to deliver his desperate message.

The Captain could see that the wagons and horses were missing from the stables. He turned to his Lieutenant and told him, "Go back to town, get the reinforcements, then head west toward Loganville and Stone Mountain, they can't be more than one day ahead of us."
"You bet, Captain," said the Lieutenant. Then the three remaining men rode off back to town to rally more men for the hunt.

Slowly, the Captain walked his horse through the mud toward the bloodbath that awaited him. As the Captain surveyed the carnage, he could only wince. He tethered his horse to a tree. As he walked up the steps and across the front porch, he noticed that the flies had already started feasting on the rotting flesh of the bodies that occupied the front portion of the house.

Vengeful Spirits

As he walked out the back door, after having inspected the house and having seen the burned remains of Gregory, he mumbled to himself, "These guys are nothing but animals." He walked back to the front of the house to retrieve his mount.

He rode the horse to the stables and put his faithful friend in a stall with some fresh hay and oats he found lying on the tack room floor. Dusk was rapidly approaching. He climbed up into the hayloft to sleep until General Sherman arrived, probably in the morning.

At dawn, he was startled awake by gunfire that sounded like thunder. Grabbing his rifle, he went to the loft door and peered out into the orange light of dawn. He saw nothing, no horses, no men, no rifle smoke. Rolling back over, he decided to wait until the others arrived. "Maybe it was just a dream," he said to himself.

A short time later he heard the sound of hoof beats. Carefully he looked out the door to see General Sherman himself riding quickly across the pasture. The Captain climbed down from the loft, mounted his horse, and rode to the house to meet the General. When he arrived at the front of the house, he was shocked at what he saw.

General Sherman himself was kneeling over the body of Miriam, whose head was missing. As the

General stood and turned around, he could see tears rolling down his bearded cheeks.

At that moment, a scout rode up and carefully approached the General saying, "Sir, Confederate soldiers are coming."

"How many are there?" asked the General.

"It looks to be only four, sir. It also looks like they have a General with them."

The six soldiers with General Sherman turned their horses and readied their weapons. Quickly, Sherman exclaimed, "Wait! Don't show any aggression unless they do first. There has been enough blood shed on this soil as it is." The soldiers lowered their weapons, but stayed ready.

General Johnston rode up from the south pasture with three men in tow. They rode up slowly with their hands up. As they approached the front of the house, General Sherman was standing in front of his men.

Johnston said, "General Sherman, we do not come as soldiers, but as mourners."

Once Johnston dismounted his horse, his men followed suit. Johnston unbuckled his sword and pistol and laid them in the dirt. Slowly, his men did the same. As if a reflection in a mirror, Sherman and his men followed Johnston's example.

The two rival Generals shook hands and discussed how they both knew the Wells couple. After an hour, the conversation was drawing to a close. Both men decided the Wells deserved a proper burial with respect and honor.

The Generals corralled their men together and instructed them to work together to bury the bodies of the slaves, including the one in the house. Surprisingly, there was minimal arguing as the men slowly and carefully started hauling bodies toward the slave quarters and digging graves there.

Sherman and Johnston worked side by side and dug two graves near the magnolia tree that shaded the front yard. Once the bodies of Josiah and Miriam were covered, large granite rocks were placed as headstones. General Sherman walked to the side of the house and picked three red roses and placed them on Miriam's grave. As he knelt over the grave, he whispered to himself, "I'm so sorry, Miriam. I should have been there."

Finally, he slowly rose, wiping tears from his eyes, and said to Johnston, "You are a true gentleman to put your differences and your aggression aside to pay homage to these two wonderful people, in the presence of your enemies."

Johnston put a hand on Sherman's quivering shoulder and replied, "You not only speak of me, but of yourself as well. For you have done the same as I have." Dusk was quickly approaching. The Generals, along with their soldiers, pitched their tents on grounds that previously Confederate troops and Union troops had fought, but now these enemies shared the battlefield and slept peacefully.

In the morning, the two Generals and their men loaded up their mounts and moved out as both Generals tipped their Stetsons to each other. Sherman stopped by Miriam's grave to say one last goodbye as Johnston and his men rode south through the tree line to rejoin the war at hand.

After the battle of Atlanta, as Sherman continued to push toward the sea, he received a letter from Washington informing him that all but two of the bummers had been captured about five miles southwest of Loganville. All six were tried and hanged for their social and military crimes. The two men unaccounted for were a man named James and the supposed leader Thomas Stringer. The men were never found, and therefore, never prosecuted, and were presumed dead.

The war was now over. General Lee had surrendered at Appomattox in September 1865. The south was putting its lives back together piece by piece. The dead were honored, wives and children mourned their husbands and fathers. Slowly, houses were rebuilt, as well as shops and businesses. There was rumor that General Nathan Forrest was starting a secret society called the Ku Klux Klan in Tennessee, but not much was known of it yet.

Years later Joe Johnston read in the paper that William Sherman had died. Remembering the short and rare bond the two men shared during the war, he rode to the funeral to pay his respects to the man he feared toward the end of the war, yet still respected as a General. Weeks later, after having stood in the rain to pay his respects to the once great General, he caught pneumonia and died himself at the age of 82.

In Madison, the only business that was not going to be rebuilt was Josiah's dry goods store. A few months prior to the war, Josiah sold the store to a friend. That friend was killed in the chaos that took place when Sherman's men swept through town. So now the brick husk that was once a thriving business and social centerpiece sat crumbling as the businesses around it began to reshape. The news of the murder of Josiah and Miriam had spread quickly through town. Even though other plantation owners had been killed, the Wells were the most prominent and well known.

Chapter Six

In Marietta, Georgia, the brother of Josiah, Preston Wells, sat in his small house just outside of town and held the letter he had received a few months ago. The letter told him of his brother's murder and his inheritance of the Wells plantation. Before now, it was unsafe to travel any distance due to the dangers of the war. Now that the war was over, travel was once again safe. Preston packed a bedroll and his pistol, along with a canteen of fresh water, for his trip to Madison to tie up the lose ends his brother had left behind.

The ride to Madison was quiet, but heartbreaking. Farms were burned and fields were decimated. Dead cattle and horses rotted in stinking lumps that brought tears to Preston's eyes. With effort, Preston drew his attention away from the sad sights he passed and tried to enjoy the colorful beauty of the leaves that were left on the hardwood trees that had not been ruined.

The November air was cool and for the first time in a long time he could remember he didn't smell smoke and hear the screams of dying soldiers.

Around Dacula, he came cross a woman and her daughter in a wagon. The wagon was sitting in the middle of the road with a missing rear wheel. The wheel was lying in the ditch next to the road. As he approached the wagon, he noticed the woman crying with her head in her hands.
"Excuse me, ma'am," Preston greeted. The woman looked up, her eyes were red and puffy from the tears of frustration she had shed. Her daughter was sitting next to her, eyes wide with fear.

The woman pleaded, "Please, sir, can you help me? I'm on my way to Athens to live with my family. They and my daughter are all I have left."
"Where's your husband?" asked Preston.
Again she began to sob, "He was a Captain with the Blue Ridge Rangers and was killed in the Battle of Kennesaw Mountain. Our house was burned, so, little Angie and I have been staying with friends until now."

Preston dismounted his horse and fished in his saddlebag and pulled out an iron pin, "I have just what you need." With the woman's help, he remounted the wheel onto the wagon and used the pin he had to secure it to the spindle.

When he was finished, he leaned against the wagon and wiped the sweat from his face with his shirt.

"Where are you going?" asked the woman.

"I am on my way to Madison to see my brother's estate. He and his wife were murdered in June, and I am just now able to travel there, to tend to the estate my brother left me in his will."

The woman looked at the ground and said with sincerity, "I'm sorry to hear of your loss. I've heard of a place in Madison that was called the 'Pasture of Grace'".

"Yes!" exclaimed Preston, "that's the place".

"You must be proud of your brother for the courage and generosity he showed to the soldiers."

"Yes, he was a good man. Do you mind if I ride along with you and your daughter for a bit?" asked Preston.

"That would be nice," responded the woman.

Preston helped the woman back into her wagon, and with a snap of the reins she started on her way. Preston rode along side of the wagon and traded small talk about family and the war. Preston was glad for the company and so was she.

About ten miles shy of Madison, the trail split. The trail north went to Athens, and the trail continuing east went to Madison. Both Preston and the wagon paused at the split.

"Well this is where we part ways, I guess," said Preston.

"Thank you for fixin' the wagon and the company," responded the woman.

"You're welcome. I hope you have a safe trip to Athens, and good luck."

"Bye, mister," said little Angie. Preston smiled and waved goodbye to the two of them and continued on his way.

As Preston trotted into town, he noticed that the devastation wasn't as bad here as it was in Marietta. For that he was glad. Maybe his brother's place wasn't too bad off after all.

He found the courthouse in its last stages of being rebuilt. It sat in the middle of town on the square. The new windows were installed, the front doors were hung, and the interior was completed.

There were a few men cleaning up outside as Preston got off his horse and tethered it to the pole next to the watering trough. He stepped inside the new building marveling at the newness and the smell of fresh lumber.

"You look lost," said a voice. Preston turned and saw a man standing in a flannel shirt with overalls and boots. His gray beard and thinning hair gave him a wise look.

"My name is Preston Wells. I'm here on behalf of my brother Josiah's estate. I'm looking for Judge Naugle. Do you know where I can find him?"

"You found him," responded the man.

Preston took a good look at the man and said, "You don't look much like a judge."

The man presented his hand and said, "It's nice to meet you. My name is Judge Rodger Naugle."

With a sheepish grin, Preston returned the handshake and said, "I'm sorry. I was expecting the Judge to be wearing a robe."

Rodger chuckled and responded, "When I'm not in court, I don't wear my robe. Right now I am helping to finish my new courthouse. That's why I'm wearing my work clothes today." Preston nodded his understanding, and Rodger continued saying, "So, you are Josiah's brother, huh?"

"Yes sir. I got the letter that you sent me, but until now I have been unable to safely travel from Marietta to respond."

"That's no problem, I'm sorry to hear about your brother and sister-in-law."

"Thank you, Your Honor."

"Please, call me Rodger. Court is not in session. Let's go to my chambers, I have some papers for you to sign."

Rodger's chambers were the first thing rebuilt, apparently. The walls were glossy oak, and the furniture was plush and new. The massive desk looked like cherry wood that shined as the sunlight poured in from the stained glass window. The center of the floor was covered with what looked like a handmade rug. It's variety of dark colors complemented the room perfectly.

"Please sit down", Rodger motioned to a wingback chair that sat in front of his desk. As Preston sat, Rodger said, "Luckily, all of our legal papers were saved from Sherman's wrath. A few days before the troops moved through we loaded our vault with everything we could. The vault and outer walls were all that were left standing when the smoked cleared after Sherman left."

Rodger handed Preston a stack of papers, "These are yours to keep. There's a property description, tax papers, and the deed to the property and the house. These you need to sign."

"What are these?" asked Preston.

"The top one is you claiming the plantation, the bottom one is the changing ownership of the property and house." Preston sighed and signed both sheets and pushed them back across the desk to Rodger.

"Okay, that's it," said Rodger.

"Can I ask you a question, Rodger?"

"Sure, shoot."

"What exactly happened to Josiah and Miriam?" Rodger leaned back in his chair and let out a long sigh.

"Do you really want to know the details?"

Preston considered how much he really wanted to know then said, "Yes. I need to know......... everything."

Rodger knew the story all too well. One of General Johnston's men had rode into town and reported the slaughter at the Wells plantation in detail. The court

Vengeful Spirits

recorder had taken down everything the soldier had said. Now sitting in his chair, Rodger recounted every last detail he could remember. In shock, Preston gripped the arms of the chair with sweaty palms. In conclusion, Rodger said, "Everyone was buried on the property, even the slaves."

Preston thought a minute, and then asked, "What about the two men that got away?"

"You mean Stringer and James?"

"Yeah, what happened to them?"

Rodger looked a bit embarrassed and quietly said, "They were never caught. The conclusion is they either died while carrying out their deeds, or they starved to death in the wilderness. They were reported to have never returned home, and haven't been heard from since."

Preston said in a defeated voice, "I guess if they haven't been found yet, they never will be."

Rodger stood up and walked around his desk as Preston stood up. Rodger placed a gentle fatherly hand on Preston's shoulder and said, "I might never get a chance to convict and sentence those two, but rest assured the Lord God Almighty will some day, and His wrath is greater than anything I can do to them."

Preston put on a smile of thanks that he really didn't feel. "Rodger, could you do me a favor, and ride with me to the estate? I don't know where it is."

Rodger grabbed his hat and said, "Sure, but I can't stay long. I have an engagement back here in about an hour."

Preston smiled and said, "Thanks. I just didn't want to ride out there alone, if you know what I mean."

As the men walked through the new oak front doors, Rodger said, "Yeah, I know what you mean. I really liked Josiah, and his wife was a true southern belle. I would be proud to lead the way."

Chapter Seven

As the men rode out of town, neither spoke. Rodger was in the lead, taking Preston to the "Pasture of Grace". Preston quietly rode listening to the clip-clop of the shoed horses trotting on the hard packed Georgia clay. Thoughts and memories of his brother flashed passed his mind's eye like still framed photographs being shuffled in his head. *What will I see when I get there?* He wondered to himself.

They rode down a rutted lane that led to the plantation. Preston's heart began to race. Through the leafless trees he could make out the white mass that was the mansion. They stopped just passed the wood line and Rodger said, "Here it is. The place is still a bit beat up. Miriam and Josiah didn't get a chance to repair much after the three day skirmish that took place here." Preston got off his horse and looked around.

"I have to get back to town for a meeting. Are you staying here tonight?"

Preston turned to Rodger on his horse and responded, "Yeah, but I can't stay at the house. It looks a bit drafty. Has the hotel in town been put back together yet?"

"It's not completely finished, but they have a few rooms available. I'll go ahead and get you a room when I get back to town. It's across the square from the courthouse."

"Thanks, Rodger. I appreciate your hospitality."

Rodger waved and said, "Don't mention it, I'll see you later."

After Rodger rode off, the plantation was still and quiet except for the rustling of leaves that littered the ground. As Preston surveyed the plantation, he saw lots of farmland separated by tree lines. There were slave quarters here and there and large oak and magnolia trees were scattered around the house with pine trees making up the tree lines.

At the northern end of the pasture, he saw what looked like hundreds of mounds with sticks growing out of them. He wondered to himself, *was my brother growing trees on his property?* To soothe his curiosity, he mounted his horse and rode over to investigate.

As he got off his horse, he realized what he was looking at. "This is a cemetery," he said to himself. "I wonder who all these people were." It was late in the afternoon, but still a fog started to crawl its way across the graves toward his feet.

"They were Confederate soldiers," said a voice from behind him.

Quickly, he spun around and his horse scampered off back toward the house. With icy fear running through his veins, he asked, "Who are you and how do you know who's buried here?" As Preston looked at the stranger, he noticed he was holding a rifle. His clothes were dirty and torn, his shoes had holes in them, and his beard was dirty and unkempt. Then he noticed that the man was somewhat transparent. The fog slowly rolled around Preston's feet, as he waited for the stranger to reply.

"I am a friend of your brother. I was here when these men were killed. That's how I know." The man pointed to a magnolia tree in front of the house, "There are two more graves you might be interested in."

Preston's gaze followed the pointed finger, "Who is buried there?" Preston asked. There was no answer. He turned to ask the question again, but the stranger was gone, along with the fog that had covered the ground. Preston spun around looking in all directions trying to see where the man had gone. There was no trace of anybody but him in sight. Suddenly it struck him, *I just saw a ghost.* The thought shook him. He had never been one to believe in such things, but now how could he deny what just happened.

Preston stood among the fallen leaves and dead branches lying on the ground. His whole belief system had crumbled. The shallow convictions and thoughts he had held his whole life were no longer in his grasp, instead they slipped through his fingers like sand. Preston was frozen in place. His mind desperately trying to grasp what just happened. His rational mind got a foothold on him, and he decided that he must have been daydreaming. "Get a grip on yourself, Pres. You're under a lot of stress. It wasn't real."

Once he had convinced himself that it was all his imagination, he turned and started walking toward the huge magnolia tree that the stranger had pointed to. Along the way, he collected his horse and tethered it to the branch of a tree.

Preston approached the magnolia and the two graves under it. He noticed the two crude granite headstones that were placed at the ends of the mounds. They had letters painted in black on them. The left one read, **M.W./R.I.P.**, and the right one read, **J.W./R.I.P.** As he knelt on the ground, he said, "I have a friend who can make y'all some nice markers, instead of just having these rocks." Suddenly a breeze picked up, and dried leaves went rustling across the graves.

As he watched the leaves roll and tumble, he heard a voice say, "That would be nice, thank you".

The voice was so faint he thought it was his imagination again. He turned around to see if another stranger was standing behind him, instead he saw the misty forms of his brother and sister-in-law.

Preston gasped and said, "Oh, no. Not again."

As he looked at both of them, he heard the voice say, "I love you little brother." The image of his brother was smiling and the figure of Miriam waved. Slowly the apparition began to dissolve into nothingness. Preston sat on the ground with his knees up to his chest and started crying. *It happened again,* he thought to himself.

"This can't be real. Maybe if I get up and walk around, I'll feel better," he said aloud. Preston stood up and took one last look at the two graves. Everything was back to normal, the leaves were still rolling across the graves, but no voices spoke.

The house stood like a victim waiting to be questioned. It was late in the day and the magnolia and oak trees cast their shadows against the sullen structure. Preston made his way up the front steps to the porch.

The recent rains had washed away most of the blood that had pooled during the murders. The bits of flesh that had littered the porch from the execution of the slaves were also gone, eaten by the local birds and rodents. There was still a faint pink stain on the right side of the porch in front of a broken rocking chair. Preston assumed that is where Miriam's head and body had come to rest. He recalled the details that Rodger had told earlier in the day while in his office. Preston looked up at the Widow's Walk and saw two knots made of rope still tied to the railing.

His pulse raced as he tried not to imagine the horror that the two must have felt moments before they were thrown off the Walk. The thought sent chills down his spine and caused a heaviness in his heart.

He turned his attention to the front door; he stepped forward and opened the creaking door. As he stepped inside, the smell of mold and dust attacked his nostrils. There were other smells under those normal scents, the faint smell of medical supplies, and an acidic burned smell. The house for the most part was okay, but it was obvious that items were missing. The rugs and pictures were askew. There were pieces of furniture missing, and the liquor cabinet was empty with its doors swung open.

Preston walked down the hall and stepped into the dining room. The dining table was broken into pieces, and he noticed a big burned spot on the wooden floor. Suddenly without warning, the room filled with smoke and in the middle of the burned spot, was a body burning. The stench made him gag, and the smoke burned his eyes. He reached up to rub his eyes and cover his nose. With his eyes shut and his nose covered, he could hear the hissing and crackling of burning flesh. As quickly as it had started, it stopped and was gone. Preston opened his eyes and uncovered his nose. The hissing and crackling noises were gone. There was no fire, or any trace of smoke except for the smell that had stuck to his clothes.

Fear took a complete hold of him, as he stood in the doorway shaking like a frightened child. *Things like this aren't supposed to happen, especially to me.*

Vengeful Spirits

After a few minutes, he regained control of himself. *Nothing has happened to me yet. Maybe the ghosts are showing me what happened. Maybe everything will be okay.* Trying to remember what Rodger had told him, he strolled to the rear of the house to look into the food preparation room. As he stood and studied the room, he heard a scratching sound and the smell of something dead. He remembered Rodger hadn't said anything about the rear of the house. With a sense of relief, he sighed, and said with confidence, "Finally, something normal. It's just mice."

With renewed confidence, Preston mounted the stairs. He could tell by the orange light streaming through the window that dusk was not far off, and he needed to hurry.

On the second floor, he found Josiah's office. It had been completely ransacked. All the furniture had been broken to splinters, and the pictures were torn and broken. Even his brother's certificates were torn and the frames broken on the floor. He sifted through the debris and retrieved the half dozen torn honors his brother had achieved. As he turned to leave the office, he noticed a hole in the far wall. He stumbled over the pile of broken furniture and realized it wasn't a hole in the wall, it was a small safe. The door of the safe was swung open. It had been emptied. He looked inside and noticed a piece of paper. He reached in, grabbed the paper, and realized it was a lone Confederate bill. "Well, it's not worth much now, but I'll save it as a keepsake," he said to himself.

He left the office and headed down the hall. At that moment, he heard a "BUMP" from the front of the house. Once again, he easily dismissed the noise with confidence saying, "Wow, the wind is pretty strong out there".

He found the bedroom in shambles just like the office. He stood in the doorway, looking at the room, when he heard a blood chilling scream from the Widow's Walk, then a loud "THUMP" from the front porch.

The icy fingers of fear gripped Preston's heart as it began to beat wildly and out of control. He broke out in a cold sweat and his skin became clammy. "Oh no!" he yelled. He was trembling out of control again. He got to the Walk's double doors and opened them. There tied to the rails were the knots of rope he'd seen from the front porch. He went to the railing and looked over the side. Down below he saw his brother hanging from the bottom of a rope. The other rope held nothing, but underneath the rope laid Miriam with her head missing. He noticed her head was resting in front of the broken rocking chair with her ghostly eyes staring up at him.

He sank back down to the floor. "Oh, God. No! This is too much." He was crying tears of fear and sorrow while still shaking. Just then he heard gunfire that sounded like thunder. The noise shook him, and he felt his bowels release. With fear and agony he screamed, "AAAHHHHH!" He ran down the stairs and out the front door. The apparitions were gone, but he didn't even notice. He untied his horse, hopped on, and rode like a madman back to town.

By now it was almost dark, but there was still enough light that Preston could see where he was going. Within minutes he was getting off his horse and checking into the hotel where Rodger had saved him a room.

After taking the bath he ordered, he went to his room and lay on the bed. He was beginning to calm down. The smell of fresh lumber and wet paint helped soothe his frazzled nerves. When he could finally think clearly, he decided he would sell the farmland and the house, if he could. Maybe if he didn't tell anyone what happened in the house tonight, he wouldn't have any trouble selling it. He would talk to Rodger about it in the morning.

Chapter Eight

After the night of restless sleep, Preston checked out of the hotel. He left his horse tethered to the post out front and walked across the square to the courthouse. Once inside, he found Rodger talking to two other men at the rear of the courtroom.

"Ah, Preston, my good man, good to see you again," greeted Rodger.

"Good morning, Rodger," replied Preston.

"Let me introduce you to two fine men. This here is, Hoyle Eiferd, he lives on the farm east of your place."

Preston shook his hand, "Nice to meet you."

"And this is Earl Edwards; he is the chairman for the Madison Confederate Memorial Association."

They shook hands, "A pleasure," said Preston.

"Have you decided what you're going to do with the Wells place yet?" asked Rodger.

"Well, I think I'm going to try and sell it. Taking care of that much land is more than I can handle. Besides, I'm happy living in Marietta and running my blacksmith stable. Do any of you know someone interested in buying the place?"

Rodger spoke up, "As a matter of fact, Hoyle here has spoken some interest in adding the Wells fields to his holdings before."

"Are you still interested, sir?" asked Preston.

"Indeed I am," responded Hoyle, "I don't have interest in the house or surrounding structures, but I could surely put the fields to good use."

"What are you prepared to offer?" inquired Preston.

Hoyle thought for a moment, while the others waited for his response. With a smile Hoyle offered, "How does ten dollars an acre for the entire 180 acres of usable land sound?"

Preston noticed Rodger's eyebrows rise in response and assumed it was a good offer. "That sounds fair to me," responded Preston, "as a matter of fact, if you have the money, I've got the papers, and the Judge as a witness. We can take care of this today, if you like."

"Sure," said Hoyle, as he shook Preston's hand. "Give me an hour to get the money and I'll be back."

"Okay, I'll be here," said Preston. "Well, that wasn't as hard as I thought it would be," Preston said to Rodger. "Now all I have to do is find a buyer for the house and remaining land."

Apparently the selling and buying of the farmland had wet Earl's appetite. He spoke up and said, as he cleared his throat, "I think the Wells place would make a fitting headquarters for the Association. What do you think Rodger?"

Rodger nodded his head in agreement, "I think it would be a fine idea."

"Well?" Preston asked, "What are you prepared to offer?"

Earl was obviously calculating in his head and thinking as he looked at the ceiling and floor. Finally he said with hesitation, "The Association could offer as much as twenty five hundred dollars for the remaining estate." Preston realized the house would take a lot of work and money to refurbish. He also snuck a peek at Rodger's expression of the offer and concluded that this offer was pretty good as well.

After a few moments of thought, Preston smiled, and said, "I can settle with that," and shook Earl's hand. "Oh, before I forget. Once I get back to Marietta my friend J.C. Duckett will be cutting new markers for Miriam and my brother. He will have them delivered and placed. Is that okay?" asked Preston.

"Sure, that will be fine. Give me a moment to retrieve the money from next door at the bank, and I'll be back."

After both men had left, Rodger said, "Wow, you liquidated the entire estate in a matter of minutes. That's incredible. Why are you so eager to get rid of that place, if you don't mind me asking."

"It's not that I was in a hurry to sell; it's just that I'm not a plantation owner, and I could use the money more than I could use the land, that's all."

Preston hoped Rodger couldn't notice the feeling of guilt that had swept over his face by not telling of the things that had happened the night before. Luckily, Rodger didn't seem to notice a thing. In a few minutes, both men returned and the transactions were made. All three men went their separate ways, happy with the way things went.

Preston returned to Marietta where, with the money he received from the sale of the plantation, he was able to rebuild his blacksmith stable and was ready to work again long before most of the businesses in town.

Earl had the Association repair and refurbish the house to its prior splendor. The mansion was used for the headquarters of the Association. It was also used as a banquet hall and visitor's center for years. The markers for Miriam and Josiah had been delivered and placed. They were beautiful, not only were they markers, but they were a work of art that attracted many gazers over the years. J.C. Duckett had apparently out done himself.

Even though the entire house had been renovated and restored the root cellar was never explored. The rusted metal hinges and solid doors were too much work to free up, so the outside of the metal doors only got a fresh coat of paint, and the overgrown bushes were cut back.

Even through the agony of war, the odds can be beaten and bonds can be made, but sometimes the ghosts of the tortured and murdered never forget.

October 1965

Chapter One

Clarsville, Tennessee

As Edward dreadfully walked down the hallway toward the conference room of the law offices where he practiced he noticed he was sweating. Small stains at the armpits of his shirt were now showing and his forehead was moist. Before he opened the conference room door he took his handkerchief out of his back pocket and wiped his forehead dry. There was nothing he could do about his shirt so he stuck the handkerchief back in his pocket and knocked on the door.

"Come in," came the reply.

Edward opened the door and walked in, "Good morning, gentlemen." Edward said, with a forced smile.

He knew what this meeting was about. He had recently gotten his second DUI in two years. His first DUI the law firm partners were able to sweep under the rug because he got stopped at a road block and paid his fine. Nobody got hurt and it was taken care of quietly. His second offense wasn't so easy to dispose of.

After leaving a company party and having had way too many gin and tonics, Edward ran a stop sign and into a man in his car crossing the intersection. When he failed a sobriety test he was jailed. It would have been simple if that's where it ended, but the victim found out he was a lawyer and was threatening to sue the firm along with Edward personally. The victim said he wouldn't sue the firm if he was fired from his job. Given the circumstances Edward knew the Board had no choice but to fire him.

"Have a seat Eddie," said Berry Walters, with a serious tone in his voice. Edward had known Berry for ten years. In fact, Berry was the one that had hired him right out of law school after he passed the BAR exam. The other five board members sat at one side of the glass-like polished oak conference table. None of them smiled. They wore either gray or black suits, white shirts, and black or blue ties except for Berry who wore a red tie. Edward took the red tie as a bad sign. You could always tell Berry's disposition by the color of his tie. Red was an aggressive color, therefore a bad thing for Edward.

Edward took a seat on the opposite side of the table from the board members. He straightened his tie and looked at Berry as Berry cleared his throat and said, "I assume you know why you've been called to this meeting."

Edward shifted in his seat, and swallowed hard. He would have killed for a sip of water to quench his parched throat. The sweating pitcher of fresh water sat within arms length of him, but he waited and responded, "Yes sir. I do. It has to do with my arrest and D.U.I."

"Yes, Eddie, it does. The board and I have discussed this situation at great length. While you are an asset to this firm, we cannot afford to accept the liability for what has happened. I'm sorry Eddie, we're gonna have to cut you loose."

Eddie reached over and took a clean crystal glass from beside the pitcher and filled it with the cold water that would bring relief to his desert like throat. He drank half of it immediately. He sat the half full glass down quietly, and said, "I don't like it Berry, but I completely understand. I'm sorry I put all of you in this awkward position professionally."

Berry sat back in his leather cushioned chair and said, as he looked at his Waterloo pen, "You're taking this better than I expected. Not that you are one to throw tantrums. I halfway expected you to at least try to bargain a little."

Edward leaned forward and put his forearms on the edge of the table and responded, "I knew this was coming so I planned ahead. A friend of mine from law school has a practice in Georgia. He has hired me as a co-partner in his firm."

Smiling with relief, Berry said, "Good. I'm glad you have someplace to go. I was worried you might find it hard to get hired elsewhere due to the way things ended here. Don't get me wrong, I would have given you excellent references. I'm sure the other firms would feel the same way we do about the risk."

"Thanks Berry. I appreciate what you've done for me."

Berry continued, "You're not leaving here empty handed either. You've got your retirement package, your profit sharing, this month's salary, and even your bonus from the Miller case last week. Due to the situation, though you will not receive your pension. I'm sorry. The board decided to make things look good to the plaintiff in your case. Some sort of monetary penalty had to be made. I hope you understand."

Edward thought to himself, S*hit, my pension, that's a decent chunk of change.* "Once again Berry, I don't like it, but I understand. I dug my hole and now I get to sit in it, but like you said I'm not leaving empty handed. Things will be okay…… I hope."

Berry leaned forward and raised his eyebrows, "No hard feelings Eddie?"

Eddie was a little annoyed about the pension, but he put on a smile and reached over to shake Berry's hand and said, "Of course not. You did what you had to do. I can't blame you for it. I guess this will be my last day. My calendar is clear now that the Miller case is over. I will clear my office and be gone by end of business today." Eddie stood, straightened his tie, and looked at the other stoned face board members, and said, "Good luck gentlemen." There was a grumble of response from the men from the other side of the table. Eddie turned and walked out of the conference room, closing the door behind him.

Once he got back to his office, his secretary Shirley stood up from her desk, and held out her arms to him. He accepted the embrace. Shirley had been his secretary for the past three years. There had never been anything between them sexually. For one thing, she wasn't the most attractive woman on the planet and the other Eddie was dedicated to his wife, Karen.

As Shirley released him she said, "I'm so sorry, Eddie. I'm gonna miss you. The firm's parties just won't be the same without you. On top of everything else, I have to break in a new counselor."

Eddie asked, "Do they already have my replacement?"

"Yeah, they hired him the day you won the Miller case."

"Who is it?"

With a look of distaste she responded, "Some young guy fresh out of law school. I think he's from Boston."

Eddie rolled his eyes, and said as he walked toward his office door, "Good luck."

Before he opened the door to his office, Shirley said, "Oh, by the way, Deputy Crowder is waiting for you in your office. It looked like he had a summons in his hand."

"I'll bet I know what that's about," he grumbled. "Thanks, Shirl."

Jay Duckett

At Eddie's house, his wife Karen and his daughter Morgan were cleaning things up and getting ready to start dinner. Karen was thin, but not too thin. She had shoulder length blonde hair with emerald green eyes and an infectious laugh. Morgan was the spittin' image of her mother. At age eight, she was full of questions and thought her father knew everything. Eddie had told Karen what he expected to happen at work today. At first she was worried that he would have trouble finding another job. She felt better when he told her that he had talked to Louis Ormand in Georgia, and had another job lined up. She had met Louis only once over Thanksgiving one year. He seemed like a nice enough guy so she didn't complain. It was almost 5:30; she knew Eddie would be home soon. She wanted dinner to be ready for him when he got there. Karen wanted things to be as relaxing as possible for him tonight. She knew he had had a rough day.

As she began preparing his favorite meal, pork chops and potatoes, she said to Morgan, "Sweetie, go upstairs and get daddy's slippers, and put them in front of his chair for him."

"Okay Mommy!" the little girl exclaimed as she ran up the stairs to retrieve the slippers.

As Eddie stepped into his office he saw the deputy sitting in the chair in front of his desk with his hat in his lap. As he passed the seated deputy he slapped him on the back and said, "Hey Richard. Let me guess, you have a summons for me from Alan Gordon's attorney."

Vengeful Spirits

"Good guess, Eddie," Richard said, as he handed him the summons. "How much is he suing you for?"

"It says……..holy shit! He's asking for $20,000. That damn nigger is trying to milk me. I can't afford that kind of money." Eddie plopped down in his chair and sighed.

Richard spoke up and said, "You know, the boys and I could help you with this problem."

Eddie looked over the top of the summons he was reading and said, "How do you mean?"

Richard smiled and said, "Come by the bar tonight at about 10:00 and we'll discuss it."

"Alright, I'll be there."

Richard rose from his chair and said before opening the door, "Don't worry, everything is going to work out fine." Then he turned and left the office and closed the door behind him. By 5:30 Edward had his office packed up and got into his 1964 Chevrolet Impala to head home.

When Edward got home he was greeted by his wife as he walked into the kitchen. She took off the oven mitts she was wearing and put her arms around his neck and gave him a kiss.

Morgan came bouncing across the freshly swept kitchen floor squealing, "Daddy! Daddy!" and wrapped her arms around his waist. For a moment with the two people that meant the most to him next to him and the intoxicating scent of the marinated pork chops cooling on the counter top everything was right with the world.

Jay Duckett

After dinner, Edward was helping his wife with the dishes. As he put the leftover pork chops and potatoes into a Tupperware container he said to Karen, "I have a meeting tonight at 10:00 at Smitty's."

Smitty's was a local bar that had a certain southern atmosphere that Edward and Richard both felt comfortable in. The walls were covered with old pictures of farmers and Confederate memorabilia. There were Confederate flags and neon beer signs on the walls as well. On the jukebox country music played and pool tables and dart boards were in the back room. The walls and floor were made from planks of wood that gave the bar the feel of a barn.

Karen knew what these meetings were usually about. She didn't like it, but she learned to deal with it. "Who's gonna be at this meeting?" asked Karen.

"Just Richard and me as far as I know. I shouldn't be late. We just have a few things to discuss."

Karen pleadingly asked, "You're not going to be discussing Berry or the firm are you?"

"No, no, baby. Berry has nothing to do with this. He's one of the good guys."

"Then what is this meeting about?"

"Sweetie you know that the subject of our meetings is classified and secret, but I promise you Berry will not be a topic of discussion."

"Alright forget I asked. Just be careful and don't get into any trouble."

"Yes dear," Eddie responded sarcastically. He went to the closet and grabbed his leather coat.

Morgan came running up "Daddy aren't we gonna watch Dragnet together tonight?"

Eddie felt a twinge of guilt as he knelt down to hug her, "I'm sorry princess. Daddy's got a meeting tonight. I'll be back and kiss you good night, okay? I promise."

With disappointment in her voice she said, "Okay daddy. I love you."

"I love you too, punkin'." And he gave her a kiss on the cheek.

As Eddie drove along Simpson Street he wondered to himself, *how long is it going to be before Morgan starts asking me what kind of meetings I'm going to? Will I lie or tell her the truth?* He pushed the thought away agreeing with himself that he would deal with it when the time came.

Eddie pulled up to Smitty's and found a spot right near the front door. It was a Thursday night so things were pretty slow at the bar. That probably accounted for the good parking spot. As he walked through the door Walter, the bartender, waved to him and pointed to a table in the back of the room where Richard sat sipping a draft beer.

"When you get a chance send me a draft over, will ya?" asked Eddie.

"You bet Eddie," replied Walter.

Eddie sat down at the small table across from Richard and said, "Okay. What is this about you and the boys being able to help me out with my problem?"

Richard took a slow pull from his frosty mug and smacked his lips, "I know Judge Bishop," was all he said.

Eddie looked puzzled for a moment then said, "Okay. So?"

Richard returned his look with one of disappointment, "You know the Klan looks after its own," Richard said, with a grin on his face.

Chapter Two

Madison, Georgia

The Wells plantation house was still standing. The Madison Confederate Preservation Association that had occupied the house for the past 100 years had changed its name to the Madison Historical Society. Their offices had been contained in the Wells house since 1865 when the place was bought from Preston Wells in the winter of that year. Now that the Historical Society had finished their new building on the other side of town they were moving their records, books, microfilm, and equipment out of the house and setting up shop there. The Society was planning to sell the house once they had completely moved out.

Jay Duckett

The Sons of Confederate Veterans had taken over the care of the large cemetery at the north end of the lot that the house sat on. The names of the men buried there had since been identified. New markers were placed at the graves, and a fence with stone pillars at the entrance had been erected around the cemetery. A sign was placed on one of the entrance pillars that read, "Here lies 198 Confederate soldiers that died during a skirmish that took place in June 1865 on this very plantation. The skirmish lasted three days. There were 129 Union dead that were carried away and buried somewhere outside Morgan County. The land for these courageous men was gladly donated to the Confederate Army by Josiah and Miriam Wells. The Wells' couple is also buried on this property to the west." On the other pillar the names of the soldiers were written along with their home states.

The Wells gravesite had been taken care of by the Society itself. A small fence was around their plots as well. The plaque that stood behind the plots read, "Here lies Josiah and Miriam Wells, the original owners of this plantation. They were murdered in June 1865 by Union "bummers", their bodies were laid to rest here by General Joseph Johnston, of the Confederate Army, and General William Sherman, of the Union Army. In an unprecedented effort both men worked side by side to bury the two people that meant so much to each of them for different reasons."

The house had been completely restored. Electricity had been installed in 1900 and was upgraded in 1950.

Vengeful Spirits

In 1958 central heating and air was installed at the sweating requests of the volunteers that worked for the Society. Everything else had been kept original except the roof that was replaced in 1902, and again in 1959. The house was a beautiful reminder of days gone by.

At night when there was nobody around the two rocking chairs that sat on the front porch would rock by themselves, and at other times, the sound of a single shotgun blast would echo off the trees to the south.

Chapter Three

Clarsville, Tennessee

Richard sat staring at Eddie to see his expression of the news that Judge Bishop was one of them. Eddie swallowed the lump in his throat and said, "Are you kidding me? If that's true then we've got unbridled power in this situation."

Richard smiled and said, "You see, I told you everything would be okay."

Eddie leaned back in his chair and thought a moment. Finally he sat forward and said, "If we have the law on our side then I want to teach this nigger a thing or two. I want to catch him out at night by himself and show him who he's dealing with."

Richard chuckled, "I like the way you think. Tomorrow is Friday. I'm sure he goes by and has a drink after work someplace. I know which factory he works at. I'll go talk to his supervisor tomorrow morning and get what information I can. I'll call you tomorrow around lunch and let you know what I've found out. I gotta get home before my wife kills me for being out too late. I'll cover your beer on my way out. We'll talk tomorrow."

Eddie smiled and shook Richard's hand and said, "Thanks Rich, 'til tomorrow."

On his ride home Eddie felt like the weight of the world had been lifted off his shoulders. Now he could start packing to move to Georgia, and his new and improved life. When he got home he went straight to Morgan's room, and gave her a kiss good night.

As he was closing the door to her room he heard her say, "Good night daddy."

"Good night punkin'," he responded as he shut the door.

The next morning he awoke to the smell of pancakes and sausage wafting through the air. He hopped out of bed feeling refreshed after the good nights rest. He felt like a new chapter was beginning in his life. As he sat with his wife and daughter at breakfast he broke the news, "We need to start packing to move to Georgia next week."

"Next week!" exclaimed Karen.

"Yay!" cheered Morgan.

"Yeah we can be packed and moved by late next week, can't we?"

Karen stumbled with her words, "What about your case with Alan Gordon?"

"That's what the meeting last night was about. It will be all taken care of."

Karen didn't like the sound of that. She knew how the Klan "took care" of things. "You're not getting yourself into something that you can't get out of are you?"

"Not at all, baby. Just trust me okay."

"Okay dear. I'll trust you."

Eddie stood up from the table and said, "I have to make some calls this morning so I'll be in my office."

"Okay dear. Don't forget either you or I need to go to the store to get some boxes to pack with."

"Sure. We'll go this afternoon." With that statement he disappeared into his office.

His first call was to Louis Ormand, his lawyer friend that worked in Madison, Georgia. "Hey Lou, it's Eddie."

"Eddie, how are things going?"

"Great. The lawsuit against me is being cleared up, and I plan on coming down by this weekend to find a place to live."

"That'll be great. I'm looking forward to seeing you again."

Louis had been running his own firm for several years now. He was starting to get swamped. He was looking forward to some relief with a new partner. With a new partner he could start picking up the work he had been forced to turn away previously. Louis was

Jay Duckett

about Eddie's age, but time and a poor diet had not been kind to him over the years. He had always been heavy, but now he'd grown a belly and was starting to get jowly. He had also grown a beard to hide his second chin. Regardless of his appearance, he was a true "good guy".

"By the way Lou, what kind of houses are for sale down there?"

Louis spoke carefully, "Well…..there are a few places but they're sort of small. What kind of money were you wanting to spend?"

Eddie thought a moment then said, "The house we're living in now is paid for. I expect to get about $45,000 for it, so maybe about $65,000."

"Hmm…" Lou said. "I'm not sure……"

"Wait! Hold that thought," Eddie snapped.

"What?"

"Karen has been wanting a place to set up a bed and breakfast for years. Are there any places like that around for sale at a decent price? I could get a business loan to help buy the place and we could live there as well."

Louis scratched his head, "I don't know. That's a pretty tall order. You know for $65,000 you could pretty much have your pick here in Morgan County." There was a moment of silence then Louis said, "Wait a minute. Where did I put it?" Eddie could hear papers rustling on the other end of the phone. "Ahh! Here it is. The old Wells plantation house is being sold. The local historical society has been using it for years. They recently built a new building and have moved out of the house. It says here they are selling it for $120,000. It also says it is being sold 75% furnished with original furniture that has been restored. I've seen the place; it's beautiful. It's pretty big as well. It would be plenty big enough for a B & B."

Eddie winced, "Ouch! $120,000, that's pretty steep."

"Well, you said you had $65,000 already. I would think getting a business loan for half the asking price wouldn't be too difficult. Plus, it would be a great tax write off."

Eddie thought about it then said, "I'll come see it when we get to town sometime tomorrow. Thanks Lou."

"Sure thing buddy. Hope to see you tomorrow."

Eddie hung up the phone. He sat in his plush office chair and thought for a few minutes. Slowly he pushed himself out of the chair and headed toward the door. "I guess I will see what Karen thinks of my great idea," he said to himself as he opened his office door.

Madison, Georgia

Louis hung up the phone in time for Deputy Carter to come in to his office with a knock at the door.

"Hey Louie. You got those subpoenas you called me about?"

"Yeah Alex. I sure do. Here ya go." Louis handed the deputy two folded sheets of paper and the deputy stuck them in his jacket pocket.

"Hey guess what?" asked Louis.
"What?"

"I think someone is going to buy the Wells place next week."

"Really? Who?"

"The guy I told you about, my friend from law school."

"Oh yeah. I remember you sayin' he was comin' to work with you. What is his last name? I don't remember you tellin' me."

"It's Stringer. Edward Stringer." The mention of the last name struck fear, shock and surprise in Alex. He stood in Lou's office rooted to the floor. The walls began to sway and a knot began to tighten in his stomach. His mouth went dry and he began to sweat.

He knew that name because he knew his family history. He never shared his family history with anyone. He knew that if people of Madison and Morgan County knew his family history his career would be over. *Maybe it's just coincidence. Maybe he's not from the same family.*

"Hey Alex. You okay? You look like you just saw a ghost."

Alex shook himself back to the here and now. "Yeah, I'm fine. I think I might be gettin' an early cold, that's all."

"Oh, okay," Lou said as he backed away, afraid to catch whatever Alex had. "I'll get these served right away and call it a day."

"Yeah, go home and get some chicken soup and some rest. I'd hate to have to serve papers myself."

"Thanks. Take it easy Lou. I'll see ya later." Alex quickly strode out of the office and outside with his keys jingling in his hand. Once outside he took deep breaths of the cool October air. The sweat on his forehead began to cool and helped him calm down. *What are you gettin' so excited about? It's probably not him anyway. What's the likelihood that two generations later both Carter and Stringer's grandsons would end up in the same town that their grandfathers had committed gruesome murder in, a hundred years ago?*

Once Alex had finished serving the subpoenas and summons from Lou's office he stopped by headquarters, clocked out, and told the switchboard operator he was knocking off early today. On his way home he stopped by the Phoenix for a couple of shots to calm his nerves. It was around 2:00 when he got to the bar so the crowd was light. He took his usual seat at the far end of the bar.

The barmaid, April, walked over and greeted him saying, "Hey Alex." The light in the bar was dim, but she could see that the deputy didn't look well. "You okay? You look a little rough around the edges."

Alex wasn't ready to tell April what was really bothering him so he said, "Yeah. I'm okay. Just a little stressed I guess."

"You want the usual?"

"Yeah, but make it a double though."

As she poured him a double shot of Jack Daniels Black Label, she asked, "Anything you wanna talk about?"

April was a good girl. She was single, blonde, shapely, and had a chest that made most of the patrons, single and married, stay for that one last drink just to watch her jiggle behind the counter. She wasn't your typical barmaid though. She really cared for the "regulars". She would listen as her "friends" would spill their guts about what was bothering them, or she would confiscate their keys and call them a ride home when they had one too many to drive.

She would especially take care of Alex. She and Alex had been seeing each other for the past nine months. Their relationship was very close and had gotten to the comfortable stage. When Alex would have a hard day he would usually come by for a drink before going home. Most of the time, he would just stop by to steal a kiss and make plans for the evening. April took good care of Alex not only because she loved him, but because Alex was the one who kept order in the town. She also felt safe when he was at the bar as well as him being plainly a nice guy.

Alex took a sip of his whiskey, cleared his throat, and said, "I heard someone is goin' to buy the old Wells place."
"Really?" April responded, with genuine interest.
"Yeah, the guy is a friend of Lou's from law school who is movin' here from Tennessee. He and his wife are wantin' to make it into a bed and breakfast."
"You don't sound very excited. I think a B & B would be a great idea. It would be the only one in town.

Vengeful Spirits

Madison is far enough away from everything else that you feel like the rest of the world don't exist once you're here a while. This town is a great get-a-way place."

"Yeah, I agree. We are a small town. Heck, we don't even have a K-Mart. If you want to go shoppin' at a large outlet store, you have to go to either Monroe or Athens. I guess I'm just suspicious of newcomers. Maybe this guy will be alright, and there's nothin' to worry about." Alex took the last shot of sour mash and put the empty glass on the bar. He grabbed his hat and said, "Alright, I'm headed home." As he left a five on the bar, he gave April a kiss and said, "Thanks baby," then headed for the door.

Chapter Four

Clarsville, Tennessee

Eddie found Karen in the laundry room. She had already taken Morgan to school and had started on her daily routine. He stood in the doorway and watched her quietly a moment. He liked the way she looked in the warm-up pants she was wearing, they were tight in all the right places. As she turned around to grab the detergent, she jumped and screamed at his unannounced presence, smiling in the doorway.

"You scared me. How long have you been standing there?"

"Long enough," he replied as he stared her up and down with a smile on his face.

She started the washing machine and asked, "Are you ready to go box hunting?"

"Sure, but first I want to ask your opinion on something."

"Okay, about what?"

"Remember you telling me you wanted to do the B & B thing?"

"Yeah," she responded with hope in her voice.

"Well, I think I found us a place where we could do that in Madison."

Karen's face lit up, "Are you serious?" she asked with excitement.

Eddie held up his hand, "Hold on now. I haven't even seen the place. Louis just told me about it this morning. I was thinking we could drive down and check it out Saturday. What do you think?"

"Oh, I can't wait! I hope everything works out. This would be a long time dream come true for me."

"Like I said, I haven't seen it yet, but Louis tells me it's one of the oldest plantation houses in Madison. The historical society has been using it since the end of the Civil War. Regardless of what happens we will need to find a place to live before next week."

Karen said with excitement, "Let's go get some boxes so I can get started packing."

As Karen was hounding the stock boy at the Piggly Wiggly about boxes, Eddie waited outside on the sidewalk. He watched as the cars and people went by. He saw Richard pull up in his cruiser and park. Eddie walked over to the driver's window and said, "Hey Rich, what's up?"

Vengeful Spirits

Richard smiled, "Oh plenty. Your problem? He walks to work because he hasn't gotten his car back from the body shop yet."

"Okay..." Eddie said, not sure what good this information was.

"Just listen," said Richard. "On Fridays he stops by this bar called, "The Blue Soul", for a drink on his way home after work. He only lives about three blocks from the bar."

"The Blue Soul?" asked Eddie. "Yeah, it's that nigger bar at the edge of town in the industrial district."

"I've heard of it, but I've never seen it," responded Eddie.

"Well, I just drove by there. There's an alley next door to the bar. It should be completely dark at night. What are you doing tonight?"

Eddie smiled, "Sounds like I'm gonna solve my problem tonight." Both men laughed and shook hands.

Richard said, "Meet me at the station at dark. You can follow me over there in your car so you can get home after the job is done. I'll be sure to be the responding officer to the call once he's found. Make sure you make it look like a mugging. He lives alone and does not have any family so we don't have to worry about family members stirring things up afterwards. Things should go smooth as silk."

Eddie slapped Richard on the shoulder and said, "I'll be there. Thanks for the help." Eddie stood up and Richard drove away.

Karen stuck her head out of the door of the grocery store and called, "Eddie, can you help me with these boxes?"

Madison, Georgia

When Alex got home he went straight to the basement. He ran down the stairs and flipped the switch at the bottom. The only light was from the naked bulbs hanging from the ceiling by their own power cords. Alex stumbled over the piles of junk that had accumulated over the years. Boxes of old pots and pans, bigger boxes of books that were supposed to be sold at the garage sale that never happened, and a pile of scrap lumber he used for his wood working hobby. He finally got to the dark corner where things hadn't been touched in years.

He started digging through the tangle of fishing poles, torn umbrellas, canoe oars, and baseball bats. There at the bottom of the pile was the box he was looking for. He reached down and pulled out the one box that was taped closed. The sides were bulging but were still able to hold its contents without breaking. Carrying the box with both hands, he walked over to the cluttered work bench. He pushed aside the box of nails, the hammer, and the drill he used to make the birdhouse, that was now rotting as it hung from a branch in the back yard. He reached up and pulled the string that turned on the fluorescent tube that hung from above the work bench. Pulling out his pocket knife, he cut the tape from the top of the box. He knew what was in the box because he was the one who packed it two years ago after his father died from a heart attack. His mother was still alive, but he had packed up this box of family history to keep it safe.

Vengeful Spirits

As he opened the box, he folded the ears down. The first thing he saw on top was a white hood and robe with the Klan's patch on it. He gently and respectfully set them aside. He knew what they were because he had the same outfit in his closet upstairs. Underneath that was a silver serving tray. When he first saw the tray as a young boy, he didn't understand why his dad kept a piece of silver with someone else's initials on it. The initials *M.W.* were engraved in the center, and had ornate engraving around the edges. He knew his last name didn't start with a W, so he didn't know whose it was. When he asked his father about it, all he said at the time was, "I'll tell you the story when you get older." As a kid, he accepted the answer and forgot about it. As a grown man, when his father's health issues were getting more serious, he and his father sat down over a few beers and he was finally told the chilling tale of what his grandfather had done and where the silver serving tray had come from. At the same time, his father showed him a box of papers, letters, and newspaper clippings he collected over the years. Some were original documents that his father had kept.

Alex slowly and carefully withdrew the tray from the box. He set it on top of the robe and hood. He ran his fingers across the surface of the tray thinking of all the places that it had been before it got to him. He reached in the box and pulled out a letter that his father had kept. The letter was from his grandfather, James Carter, to his grandmother, Lola. It was dated July 1865. The letter told his wife that he had bought a house near Stone Mountain, Georgia and gave her directions on how to find it. He wrote that things had gone bad during the war, and Union military officials were after him and his friend, Thomas for things they had done in the recent past. He continued by writing that he could not return home because of his fear that the law would be waiting for him. He didn't want to involve her or his son to any hostilities should it come to that. Apparently, there was some Confederate money with the letter for travel expenses. He told her she would know it was the right place if there was a silver platter hidden inside the pantry. He told her he had hidden some Confederate money under the floor boards in the bedroom. He finished his letter by apologizing and telling her he loved her and his son. He hoped he could return to his new home in Georgia, but if that didn't happen the best thing she could do for her safety was to live under the assumption of a war widow. The letter was signed, "Your loving husband, and your sons father, James Carter".

Alex had done some research of his own and the only information he could find on Thomas Stringer was that he was from Ohio and that the last time he showed up on a muster roll was in April 1865, just south of Charlotte, North Carolina.

Clarsville, Tennessee

Karen and Eddie got back home with their car load of boxes about 3 p.m. Eddie helped Karen take the boxes in the house. For the rest of the afternoon, they packed things up from closets, the cupboards, and the attic. They had stopped by and picked up Morgan on

Vengeful Spirits

the way home so she was doing what she could to help out as well.

After a dinner of frozen pizza and salad, Karen said, "I've had enough packing for one day. I think I'm gonna sit on the couch, relax, and watch some t.v. You wanna watch Gunsmoke with me?"

Eddie hated to tell her no, but he had a very important meeting with Mr. Gordon tonight. "There's nothing I would like more, but I've got a meeting tonight."

This time it was Karen who protested, "Another meeting? You just had one."

Eddie put his hands up as if to stop the words from pummeling him. "I know baby. This should be the last meeting for a good long while. The boys and I just need to tie up some loose ends before we move. Okay?"

"Will you be late?"

"I hope not, but I can't guarantee I'll be home before Dragnet goes off."

With an exasperated sigh she said, "Okay, just be careful."

"I will."

He leaned down and kissed her on the cheek. Morgan was on the floor watching the beginning of Gunsmoke. She didn't even notice Eddie leave.

Chapter Five

Eddie pulled up to the sheriff's office. Richard was sitting in his car waiting. "You ready to go settle things?" Richard asked as he leaned out of his window.

Nervously, Eddie answered, "As ready as I'll ever be."

"You follow me to where we will leave your car. It's a dark parking lot. No one will notice you."

Eddie gave Richard the thumbs up. Then Richard took off in the lead. As the two men drove across town, Eddie checked his front seat for the brass knuckles and change of clothes he brought along for the event. Richard pulled into the Rexall Drugs parking lot. Eddie pulled in behind him and parked in the darkest corner he could find. He got out of his car and walked over to Richard's cruiser idling in the dark with the headlights off.

Richard leaned out of his window and said, "The Blue Soul is two blocks that way," as he pointed out the window.

"There's an alley next to the bar. There are no lights in the alley, and the streetlight is out as well. You should have no problem taking care of business quickly and quietly. As soon as the job is done, walk back here to your car, change clothes, and drive back home. I'll take care of the rest. Be sure to burn the clothes you're wearing when you get home." Richard drove off into the night leaving Eddie in the darkness of the parking lot.

Cautiously, Eddie walked down the sidewalk toward the bar looking for possible routes he could take if things went south. The October air was chilly and it was overcast so there weren't many people out and about to observe him. Even on a warm night this is not the side of town you wanted to be in after dark. As Eddie turned the corner at Maple Street, he could see the blue neon sign that announced the Blue Soul.

As he approached the bar, he noticed a couple of black men coming out of the front door. Quickly, he ducked between two cars parked at the curb. The two men were talking and laughing loud enough that he could tell they were crossing the street and moving down the block away from him. Slowly, he stood up and approached the building. From inside, he could hear a live blues band playing. He walked up to the side of the bar and peered through a dirty window. The place was small. Only one room with a bar facing the window he was looking through. It was dark enough outside that he was sure nobody inside could see him. He searched for

Vengeful Spirits

the face of Alan Gordon among those at the bar. There he was at the far end. He was sitting alone. That was good. If he was drinking alone then he would possibly leave alone. Now that he knew Alan was still inside, he slowly backed away from the window and went around the building to wait in the alley.

It was a little after eleven when he saw Alan exit the bar and head his way. Eddie backed up around the corner and waited. His hand tightened its grip on the brass knuckles. All of his senses were alert. He could hear the music from inside. He could smell the stale beer and cigarette butts from the dumpster behind him. He could feel his heart racing in his chest. Now as Alan neared the alley he could also hear the soles of Alan's shoes crunch the dead leaves and litter that covered the sidewalk. Just then Alan's silhouette appeared at the mouth of the alley.

With the speed of a cobra, Eddie grabbed Alan's coat collar with one hand and struck his head with his other hand that held the brass knuckles. He held onto the coat and threw him to the ground toward the back of the dark and littered alley. As Alan hit the ground, Eddie heard bottles rolling across the alley. He heard Alan moan then heard a bottle break. In the darkness he saw the shadowy figure of Alan's arm swinging his direction. The broken bottle that Alan had picked up and swung at Eddie caught him in the leg. Suppressing a scream of pain, Eddie struck back with a kick that connected with Alan's chin. He heard Alan's mouth snap shut as he fell backwards to the ground. The wound inflicted on his leg by the bottle ignited further rage and hatred toward this "no good nigger". Eddie had lost control. What was supposed to have looked like a common mugging was quickly turning into a bloodbath.

He knelt down over him and started pounding at his head with the brass knuckles, with frightening speed. Still on his back Alan tried to defend himself while, at the same time, tried to attack. It seemed like the more he struggled the harder he got beat. Eddie kept up his mindless attack. Finally, he could feel his hand getting wet and warm. His mind took control and he stopped. Breathing hard, from his exertion, his breath was steaming in the cool night air. Still hunched over Alan Eddie could see what was left of Alan's face and head. He looked at his hand with the brass knuckles still gripped tightly.

There was blood and bits of flesh stuck between his fingers. As Eddie looked at his shirt, he noticed it also was splattered with blood. He looked down at the lump of raw meat that had been Alan's head and saw blood bubbles forming where his nose had been. Eddie stood up and started to walk out of the alley then turned around and gave one last kick to Alan's ribcage to stifle the constant groaning. As his foot made contact, through his shoe, he could feel Alan's rib crack. With the adrenaline fading away, Eddie reached down and took Alan's wallet, cash, and keys from his pockets.

Alan laid in the alley bleeding. Once the beating had stopped, he thought someone would come to help,

Vengeful Spirits

but help never came. He couldn't take any more. His body was going numb. Then like a shot from a cannon, he was kicked one last time. He felt his ribs crack as his bones snapped at the impact of the kick. Next he felt his pockets being rifled. His mind finally gave into the pain and shut down into unconsciousness.

Eddie heard the music stop and people start cheering. He quickly trotted across the street between two buildings and waited a moment. He saw a man with a trash bag exit the bar and step into the alley. "Oh shit!" He heard the man yell as he dropped the bag. Quickly, the man ran back inside. This was Eddie's cue to git. He quickly walked down the block between the two buildings and crossed the street. Ten minutes later he arrived at his car. He could hear in the distance the siren of an ambulance. He looked around to make sure nobody had seen him trot back to his car. He pulled off his coat and slid behind the wheel. Once he cranked up his car, he changed his clothes and wiped his hands clean with his dirty, bloody clothes.

While changing his pants, he checked his leg. It wasn't bleeding as bad as he feared. It was just a nick. He wouldn't even need stitches. At that moment, he saw the red light from Richard's squad car and heard the siren. As Richard passed, he looked in Eddie's direction and kept going.

When Eddie got home, Karen and Morgan were asleep. He took the bloody clothes and threw them in the fireplace, and watched as all of the evidence went up in smoke.

Chapter Six

Madison, Georgia

Alex sat on the stool at the workbench and thought to himself, *how do I find out who this Edward Stringer guy is? I need to find out where his family is from.*

The sound of April opening the door to the carport and yelling, "Al, where are you?" broke him from his thoughts.

"I'm down here," he answered. Quickly, he stashed everything back in the box and hid it on the top shelf of the wall mounted bookshelf on his left.

He turned off the lights and headed for the stairs. He was halfway up the stairs when April opened the basement door.

She looked down at him and asked, "Whatcha doin' down there? You gonna make another birdhouse? The one out back is in bad shape." With an attempt at humor she added, "the housing authority came by and condemned it. They said it wasn't safe to live in, even for birds."

Alex smiled and chuckled, "That's funny stuff. You're a riot, Alice. Yeah, I thought about the birdhouse. I think I'll wait 'til spring though." Alex had other matters on his mind right now. As he reached in the fridge to get a beer, he asked April, "Whatcha wanna do for dinner?"

Saturday was Alex's day off. At 8:00 a.m. he was sitting on the front steps of the new historical society. At 8:05 a.m. the curator of the society rolled up and parked in the spot with his name on it.

Markus Prather ambled his way up the steps and greeted Alex, "Good morning Alexander. What are you doing crowding my steps so early?"

Alex stood up as Mark fumbled with his keys. "Mornin' Mark. I just want to look through your Union enlisted soldier books. I'm doin' a little research for personal interest."

"Well, I'm not really ready for research visits like that yet. I'm still arranging files and getting everything ready, but I guess it wouldn't hurt. Lucky for you those books are already on the shelf. Just be sure you put it back when you're done."

Mark was the anal retentive type, but that's what made him perfect for his job. Over the years Alex learned to accept that part of Mark. It made dealing with him a lot less stressful.

The new building still smelled like fresh paint and new carpet. Things were more organized than he thought they would be from what Mark had said, but he had to remember that unless things were perfect, Mark thought they were a mess. Alex reached for the bookshelf with the row of blue volumes on it. He found the one that contained the enlisted men with the last name starting with "S". He pulled it from the shelf and sat down at the table nearby with 4 chairs neatly huddled underneath.

He flipped the pages to the "S" section. There were only a few Stringers, but there was only one Thomas Stringer. It showed he enlisted in 1862 and his home state was Illinois. Now at least he knew where Thomas Stringer was from. When he got the chance he would ask this guy, Edward, where his family was from. He would have to be discreet. If Edward knew as much about his family history as he knew about his he probably wouldn't want the whole town to know, especially if he planned on living here.

Clarsville, Tennessee to Madison, Georgia

After breakfast, Eddie, Karen, and Morgan all piled into the Chevy and headed out of town.

"I can hardly wait to see the place," Karen said with excitement.

Eddie looked over at her and smiled, "Like I said, I haven't even seen it yet. Lou just said it was for sale and that it would make a great B & B, that's all. It might be a real dump. I guess we'll see when we get there."

Eddie looked over his shoulder. Morgan was leaning over the front seat with her arms crossed, "Daddy, what is a plantation?"

Eddie looked back at the road as he spoke, "A plantation was what they called a place where crops were grown on lots of land and usually had slaves that worked the crops. The plantation owner had his mansion on the land as well".

"Is that where we're going to move to? A plantation? Is it daddy?"

"I don't know punkin', we'll see."

"Okay. Tell me when we get there." With her question answered she slid to the backseat and went to sleep.

The 360 mile trip from Clarsville, TN, to Madison, GA, took almost six hours. After having stopped for gas and lunch around one o'clock in Dalton, GA, they finally rolled up to the real estate office in Madison on Washington Avenue at four o'clock. Eddie and the girls got out and stretched. Eddie was hungry, but he wanted to talk to the agent first.

105 East Jefferson Street

As Eddie walked through the door of the real estate office, a bell jingled above his head. A portly woman walked into the room from a doorway in the back. She extended her hand and introduced herself.

"Good afternoon. My name is Alice Edge. How can I help you folks?"

Eddie smiled, accepted the handshake, and responded, "My name is Edward Stringer. Louis Ormand said you would be expecting me. I'm interested in the Wells' house."

As if she just remembered, she responded, "Oh yes. How wonderful. Lou said something about a B & B."

"Yes, my wife and I are considering using the place for a B & B, if everything works out."

Alice's face beamed, "The Wells place would be perfect for that. Would you like to go see the place now?"

"Yes, if it's not too late."

"It's never too late," Alice said, as she dug through a desk drawer and withdrew a key ring with several keys on it. "Shall we go?" She asked, as she waddled through the door.

Eddie and the girls followed Alice through the small town of Madison, "This is definitely a small southern town," said Eddie.

"I love it," responded Karen.

In five minutes they were turning off of Highway 83 onto a gravel driveway. There were stone pillars on each side of the driveway. Arching between the tops of the pillars was an iron banner that read, the 'Pasture of Grace'.

"Are we at the right place?" asked Karen as she looked through the top of the windshield as they passed between the pillars.

"I don't know. I'm just following our guide," answered Eddie.

As they approached the house, Karen gasped, "Oh my God!"

Morgan hung over the front seat and said, "Cool, huh daddy?"

Eddie could only squeeze, "Yep" out of his tightening throat.

He knew he'd never been here, but he had the strongest sensation of de'ja'vu. The house looked familiar somehow. As he and the girls got out of the car, his attention was drawn to the Widow's Walk. For some reason his mind's eye was showing him a view *from* the Widow's Walk looking over the front yard.

The picture he saw in his mind was a little different from what he saw in front of him. In his mind, there was no driveway and there were people clustered at the front of the house.

"Eddie!" His wife's call snapped him out of his daydream. "Aren't you going to look inside with us?"

Eddie did his best to smile. "In a minute. I'm going to look around outside a minute first."

"Okay, but don't be too long."

The girls went through the front doors and disappeared. Inside his gut, he had an urgency to go to the back of the house. Without question, Eddie quickly walked to the rear of the house. He stood just outside of the rear door. "There's nothing back here. Why did I feel the need to see the back yard?" As he turned to walk back to the front of the house, he noticed about twenty feet away there was a spot of dead grass about the diameter of a basketball, "Huh. The groundskeeper must have spilled some gas, and killed the grass." He said to himself. The rest of the yard was a lush dark green except for the one dead spot that stuck out like a sore thumb. With nothing to see, he headed back to the front of the house.

As Eddie walked through the front door, the house seemed warm and inviting. There weren't many furnishings but it had a certain warmth to it. He could hear Karen and Alice talking and Morgan running around quickly checking out everything. The house seemed plenty big for a B & B he figured, as he walked down the first floor breezeway.

He got to the rear of the house where there was a large kitchen. It didn't have all the appliances, but there was room for them. He got to the end of the kitchen and noticed a small room with appliance hookups. *This must be the laundry room,* he thought. As he stood still looking into the room, he could hear a scratching sound coming from the floor. He also caught a whiff of something that smelled dead. "Great. Mice," he said aloud. He closed the door and headed towards the upstairs.

"These rooms were used as offices, but could easily be converted back to bedrooms," Alice was saying as Eddie reached the top step on the second floor.
"Oh Eddie. Isn't this perfect? Alice says that all of the antique furniture we see comes with the house. What do you think?"

"There is central heat and air, and bathrooms have been added on both floors. The exterior walls were insulated when the house was renovated. The attic was also insulated, and a new roof was put on several years ago," Alice informed. As if reading Eddie's mind, "There's also hot and cold running water and a septic system."

Eddie felt uncomfortable talking in front of Alice.

Eddie pulled Karen a few steps away and said, "Why don't we get a place in town to stay for the night and talk about it?"

"Okay baby, we can do that."

Eddie stepped over to Alice and asked, "Do you have a listing sheet for this house? We are going to sleep on it tonight. I have some calls to make, and we're hungry and bushed."

"I sure do," beamed Alice. "My number is right at the bottom. I'll be in the office until one o'clock tomorrow. Just give me a call."

She handed Eddie the sheet, and Eddie asked, "I noticed a burn mark on the living room floor, is that going to be repaired?"

Alice cleared her throat and smiled, "We've replaced the floor boards in that room more than once. Each time the mark returns. I'm not sure why, but we had it covered with an area rug before and things were fine. We can replace the boards again, but I can't promise the mark will be gone for good."

Eddie scratched his head and looked at Karen, who didn't seem to care one bit about the mark, he decided that they would not bother with the mark and just cover the floor with a rug. "Nah, that's okay. I guess we'll just cover it up."

Alice once again smiled. "Okay that's fine. If you change your mind just let me know."

Eddie turned back to Morgan and Karen. "Y'all ready to go? It's almost dark."

Morgan piped up, "Daddy, I'm hungry."

"Me too, punkin'. Let's get something to eat."

On the front porch the two rocking chairs that had been rocking slowly stopped as soon as the front door opened. After everyone had driven down the gravel drive and disappeared, the chairs again began to slowly rock back and forth.

Chapter Seven

The next morning Eddie called Lou at home, "Hey Lou," Eddie said as he heard the line pick up, after three rings.

"Eddie? Is that you?"

"Yeah, it's me. Say Lou, I was wondering what kind of salary are you giving me?" The line was quiet a moment, "Lou, you still there?"

"Yeah, I'm still here. Why are you asking? Did you get another job offer or something?"

"No, nothing like that. I was thinking of buying a place and I need to know what I can expect to get paid."

"Well, I figured around $60,000-$80,000 a year, plus bonuses. Does that sound okay to you?"

"Yeah, that sounds great Lou."

"You say you found a house?"

"Yeah, I've decided to buy the Wells place."

"You're kidding. That's great. Have you even seen it yet?"

"Yeah, last night the girls and I went out to see it with Alice. I would have called you sooner, but it was late when we got here yesterday and we were hungry and tired. After we sign the papers, we're going to get a quick lunch. Do you care to join us? We are going to eat at Ye Olde Colonial on the square."

"Sure. What time?"

"Let's say one o'clock."

"Great. I'll see you there."

Eddie hung up the phone, and he and the girls left the motel to meet with Alice.

After meeting with Alice at the real estate office, Eddie, the girls, and Lou had a quick lunch. Lou filled them in about the town, and had small talk. By 1:45, Eddie and his family were headed out of town and back to Tennessee to bring their life to Madison.

As Lou was walking to the car to go back home, Alex honked his horn at him as he rolled to a stop behind Lou's car. "Hey Lou, what's goin' on?"

"Hey Alex, remember that friend of mine from Tennessee?"

"Yeah, Stringer, right?"

"Yeah. Well, he just bought the Wells place. They should be moving in next week."

"Hey, that's great Lou. Looks like you got a new partner after all."

"Looks like it."

Alex put his police cruiser in gear, "I gotta run Lou. Congratulations."

"Thanks, Alex. See ya tomorrow."

As Alex drove away, that feeling of foreboding and fear came over him again. It wasn't as overbearing and controlling as it was before, but it still caused a cold knot in the pit of his stomach. On a whim, he turned his car around on Main Street and took a left on Highway 83 headed out of Madison toward the Wells plantation.

Alex slowly pulled down the driveway and parked in front of the house. He turned off the engine and sat staring at the house. He could have sworn he saw the rocking chairs moving when he pulled up. Then again, it could have been the wind. Alex had never looked around the house. He had been down here before to escort visitors or to patrol on weekends or nights, but had never gotten out of the car and looked around.

Part of the reason was because of his grandfather and what he did here. He felt like he wasn't wanted here. Alex believed in the supernatural. He had never had any experiences himself, but still he believed. He decided to face his fear and test the spirits.

He opened his door and stood beside the car staring at the grand mansion and grounds. He began walking toward the Confederate cemetery. He had heard there was a cemetery on the property, but had no idea it was so large. Before he entered the gates, he read the plaque on both pillars. "Wow, almost 200 dead soldiers. The skirmish must have been a bloodbath," Alex said to himself as he slowly strode through the rows of headstones. Once he got to the middle of the stone forest, he saw a flat piece of polished granite set in the ground with an inscription. The inscription was placed by the S.C.V. and it read, "This cemetery and stone is a memorial to all of the fellow Confederate soldiers who gave the supreme sacrifice for their homeland."

As Alex knelt to read the memorial, behind him a dense white fog crept over the graves toward him. Before he was able to stand up, the fog enveloped him like a wet soggy blanket. Suddenly he couldn't breathe and he slumped over on the leaf covered grass. As he lay on the ground, his breath continued to elude him. The fog was so thick around him he couldn't see his hand in front of his face. Within the fog he heard voices, but couldn't understand what they were saying. While lying on the ground at the edge of consciousness, he could now feel hands grabbing at him all over. The air had a heaviness of dread to it. He could smell sweat, smoke, and a coppery smell that reminded him of fresh blood. The voices in the fog got louder and changed to sounds of agony and pain. The noises pushed against his eardrums to the point of pain. He began to pray that he would die just to make the nightmare go away.

As the voices rose in volume, they reached a climax of a hundred voices screaming at once, then stopped as quickly as they started. Alex opened his eyes. The fog was gone. So were the voices and smells. His heart was racing so fast, he thought he would have a heart attack. He still had a sheen of sweat on his forehead, and his palms were moist and clammy. As he stood on shaky legs, he wiped the sweat with the sleeve of his shirt. For a moment he looked around trying to figure out what just happened. The sun was still out, and the cemetery looked just as it did a few moments ago.

He turned toward the gates and began to walk quickly out of the cemetery. Just then a blast of ice cold air hit him in the face then covered his entire body. Alex froze in fear. It was so cold he could see his breath. As fear held him in place, a voice whispered in his ear, so close he could feel the icy breath. "Get out murderer!" A fear for his life broke him free, and he ran like a madman back to his car and left in a spray of gravel and the sound of his car's engine racing back to town at top speed.

Chapter Eight

Clarsville, Tennessee
Monday morning the phone rang at Eddie's house. Eddie got to the phone first. "Hello?"

"Eddie! It's Susan. I've got some great news." Susan was the real estate agent that Eddie and Karen had hired to sell their house. She lived down the street from them in the quiet single family neighborhood that they had lived in for the past six years.

"Hey Sue. What's up?"

"While y'all were out of town, I sold the house."

"Really? That's great." Eddie paused a moment, "You did get the asking price, didn't you?"

Susan laughed. "Of course, dear. You're not dealing with just any real estate agent."

Eddie smiled to himself. "You're the greatest Sue. When's the closing?"

"The closing is tomorrow at three o'clock. All we need to do is sign the papers, and that's it. Their loan has already been approved."

"Sounds good to me, there's just one thing. We won't be out of the house until Friday or Saturday. That's not a problem is it?"

"No not at all. I took care of everything. I told the buyers that they could move in by next Wednesday."

"Sue, you really are the greatest. Remind me to give you a bonus along with your commission."

Sue laughed again. "You know I will."

"Okay. Thanks again Sue. See you tomorrow at three."

"Bye Eddie."

When Eddie hung up the phone, he leaned back in his chair and laced his fingers behind his head. "For a Monday today is starting out pretty well." He scanned his office. So far his office was about half packed and boxed up. Most of the shelves were empty and his filing cabinets were securely locked up. "Well, I need to give Karen and Morgan the good news," he said to himself as he slid from the chair.

Karen and Morgan were in the kitchen packing up the pantry. The pots, pans, and dishes were all boxed up and stacked in the middle of the floor. Eddie walked into the kitchen,

"Karen!"

"I'm in here," responded Karen from the walk in pantry.

"Guess what baby? We sold the house."

With excitement Karen stumbled over the cans and jars on the floor of the pantry. "We did? That's wonderful. When do we have to be out of here?"

"There's no rush. They aren't moving in until next Wednesday, thanks to the skillful work of Susan."

Karen sighed, "Good. She really did a good job. We put the house on the market only two weeks ago. I'm really impressed. You know she deserves a bonus, right?"

Eddie smiled. "I already told her that. She'll be taken care of."

Karen hugged Eddie and said, "Everything is working out perfectly. I'm so happy and excited."

"Me too," responded Eddie. "I have to go to town to arrange for the movers. You think we can be packed up and ready to go by Friday morning?"

Karen put a finger to her lips and thought a moment. "I think so. With the three of us working we might be ready before then."

Smiling Eddie said, "Okay. I'll tell them to be here Friday morning." Eddie turned and started toward the door. "I won't be long. I'll bring back lunch for us."

"Okay baby. Be careful," responded Karen as Eddie was out the door.

As Eddie exited the Allied moving company, he saw Richard's car parked across the street. Eddie waved to Richard, but Richard only motioned for Eddie to follow him. He ran to his car and followed Richard to the outskirts of town to the city cemetery. Eddie followed Richard through the cemetery to a quiet, secluded corner of the Eternal Hills cemetery. Richard got out of his car and sat on the trunk. Eddie rolled to a stop behind him. He was starting to get worried. Why did they come out here to talk? This didn't look good at all. The small butterflies that had started in his stomach had grown to large winged bats furiously flapping their wings in the pit of his stomach.

Eddie got out of his car and sat on the hood, and said, "What's going on Rich? Everything's okay, isn't it?"

Richard looked relaxed as he pulled out a cigarette from its pack and lit it. After blowing out a puff of smoke he said, "Sure, everything's fine. Until this case is settled we can't be seen hanging out together. You could become the public's prime suspect due to the pending lawsuit. It wouldn't look good for the responding officer and the suspect to be paling around together. Even though we've got all the angles tied up, we need to keep up appearances. You know what I mean?"

Eddie breathed a sigh of relief. Knowing that everything was okay, the stress that had mounted drained out of him like a deflating balloon. Richard could see the sense of relief on Eddie's face.

He slapped Eddie on the back and said, "Yes, you can finally relax."

Madison, Georgia
Alex got back to town and went straight to the coffee shop at the city limit. He sat in the parking lot trying

Vengeful Spirits

to calm his nerves before he went in. "Holy shit!" he said to himself. "What was that all about?" He closed his eyes and laid his head back on the headrest. He remembered the fog and the claustrophobic feeling of not being able to breathe. He then remembered the hands in the fog. They were grabbing him all over. He remembered hands clamping down like vices on his wrists. He pulled up the sleeve of his jacket and saw a bruise on his wrist. "Oh my God," he said aloud. He pulled up the other sleeve, and saw a bruise on the other wrist as well. "It was real. It really happened." He pulled his sleeves back down. He leaned forward and rested his head on the steering wheel. As if his grandfather was in the car with him, he asked, "Grandpa, what the hell did you do?"

Instantly in his mind the answer came, "More than you know." Alex bolted up straight in his seat. He turned the ignition and started the car. "Coffee isn't gonna do it tonight. I need a drink." As he drove to the Phoenix, he radioed the dispatcher that he was signing off for the night. His shift was over and he needed a drink, a stiff one.

Alex took his usual seat at the far end of the bar. April came over with a cold beer from the tap and a warm kiss. "Hey baby, how was your day?"

Alex took a long sip of his beer and then said, "Better now." Alex took off his coat and hung it from the back of his chair. It was Monday night so things were slow and April was in the mood to talk.

April noticed the bruises on his wrists and asked, "Anything you wanna talk about?"

Alex took another sip of brew and cleared his throat. "What do you know about the Wells place, other than common knowledge?"

April leaned on the bar and thought a moment. "Mark has told me of times in the house where he heard footsteps in the first floor breezeway when he was the only one there. Other times he would notice cold spots in various rooms of the house. Stuff like that. Why are you askin'?"

Alex was quiet a moment, as he took another sip of beer. He studied April's face a moment, then asked, "Can I trust you to keep a secret?"

April leaned closer, "Sure."

Alex showed his wrists. "I got these this afternoon at the plantation in the Confederate cemetery."

April's face revealed her shock. "What happened?"

Alex told her what happened in every detail. When he was finished, he said, "Please don't think I'm crazy. Don't tell anyone either. I could lose my job. If the mayor hears of any of this he'll think I'm nuts. I'll not only lose my job, he'll have me committed to Maysville psycho hospital."

April smiled and patted Alex's hand. "Don't worry I won't let anyone know you're crazy."

Alex looked at her in shock. "You don't believe me?"

She laughed and said, "Yes, I believe you. I myself believe in things like that. I'm just excited to see someone experience what I believe and others scoff at, that's all."

Alex relaxed and finished off his beer.

"Can I give you some advice?" April asked.

Alex looked up at April from his empty beer mug with a questioning look.

"First, stay away from the cemetery."

Alex chuckled. "Like I haven't already thought of that."

"Good. Second, go home and get some rest. You look like hell."

Alex smiled. "You know just what to say to make a guy feel special

April gave him a quick kiss. "I'll be by later to check on ya."

Alex put a five on the bar and shrugged his coat on. As he got back to his car, he made a mental note to himself, "I need to talk to Mark at the society tomorrow."

At the Wells mansion, in the darkness of the late October air, two rocking chairs slowly rocked back and forth as two ghostly apparitions enjoyed each others company in the quiet of the evening.

Chapter Nine

Clarsville, Tennessee
As Eddie sat on the hood of his car, Richard told him the details of the past weekends events. "When I got to the scene, I was genuinely shocked. You literally beat him within an inch of his life. If I hadn't known who it was to begin with, I wouldn't have been able to I.D. him. You did a good job. To me and everybody else, it looked like a mugging that went bad. The medics were there when I arrived. They already had him on a stretcher. When I looked at him and asked the medics if they found any I.D. I saw he was pretty well bloodied up. From where his nose was supposed to be, blood bubbles kept going up and down and raw flesh was torn away to where I could see bone. It was a grizzly sight, to say the least. I followed the ambulance with lights and sirens going

until about a block shy of the hospital. The ambulance slowed and turned off its lights and siren. I knew from experience that Alan was already dead.

When we got to the hospital, I got out of the car and asked why they slowed down. The driver said that they had lost his pulse for the third and last time about the time they hit Lexington Avenue. The doctor came out of the emergency room door to the ambulance and pronounced him dead on arrival. I continued to act the part and asked if he had said anything. Both paramedics said no, he hadn't. I quickly returned to the scene to ask questions and to make sure no evidence was left behind. I looked but couldn't find anything. I questioned the other officers that had responded and the onlookers that were left. No one questioned could remember hearing or seeing anything at the time of the attack."

Richard took a moment to finish his cigarette. He dropped it on the pavement, and crushed it out under his shoe. "I must say I'm quite impressed. Even without having to pull strings, I could easily write this up as a random mugging and no one would be the wiser. You did a very good, clean job. I'm proud of you. Everybody else is convinced that is was just that, a random mugging and nothing else. Your name hasn't even been brought up."

Eddie breathed a sigh of relief. "Good. I'm glad that's over with. Karen and Morgan are at the house right now packing. We will be moving out Friday morning. I myself still have a good bit of packing to do."

"Well, I guess I'll let you get to it then." Richard said, as he slid off the trunk of his car and fished his keys out of his pocket.

Eddie stuck out his hand and shook hands with Richard. "Thanks again Rich for all your help."

Richard responded, "No problem buddy."

Both men held up their right hands toward each other and said in unison, "White power!"

Both men left the cemetery in separate directions. On his way home, Eddie stopped at McDonald's and picked up lunch for himself and the girls.

Madison, Georgia

Tuesday morning Alex walked into the new historical society building, and found Mark working at sorting rolls of microfilm into new banks of drawers that lined the wall.

"Hey Mark. Ya got a minute?"

Mark looked up from his task, "Hey Alex. Sure. What can I do for you?"

"I've got some questions about the Wells house."

Mark put the box of microfilm down and motioned for Alex to sit at the cluttered table. Mark sat and asked, "What do you want to know?"

Alex cleared his throat, "Do you have the original document of the report filed by the Union soldier at the time of the discovery?"

Mark smiled with pride, "I sure do. Why do you ask?"

"I wanna read it."

Mark stumbled on his words a moment and said, "I can't let anybody touch it. It has to be handled carefully. You must wear gloves and a mask."

Alex tried to hide his irritation. "Well then, can you read it for me?" Mark's eyes brightened.

"Sure. Follow me. We need to go to the viewing room to look at the document."

Alex followed Mark to a small room with weird lighting and a sterile smell to it. "I'll be right back," Mark said as he left the room. A few minutes later he returned wearing cotton gloves, a surgical mask, and a hair net. He looked more like he should be working at a chicken processing plant instead of the historical society. He was carrying a flat box like a pizza. He pushed the door open with his foot and set the box carefully on the table.

With the caution of a bomb squad member, he removed a yellowed sheet of paper from the box, and placed it on the table. With a grand gesture, he unfolded the paper to full length. With it unfolded completely, it was about two feet long and maybe nine inches wide. Mark stood over the ancient document and began to read, "June 27, 1865 while on follow up patrol through Morgan County, in Madison, Georgia, my men and I came across the plantation owned by Miriam and Josiah Wells.

Upon approaching the house, I noticed bodies lying on the front steps. The body of Josiah Wells was hanging from the Widow's Walk by a hangman's noose. His wife, Miriam, was the victim of a botched lynching.

Vengeful Spirits

A second rope was hanging from the walk without a body. The body of Miriam Wells was found lying on the porch under the rope. Her head was found several feet away, resting in front of a rocking chair. The front steps were littered with male slaves. All of them had been shot in the back of the head. The porch and front of the house was splattered with blood and flesh from the executions. Crows and rats had started devouring the remains.

A search of the house found one male slave in the dining room. The top of his head was missing, and his body had been set on fire. The house had been looted of all valuables, and ransacked heavily. A search of the slave quarters and surrounding grounds proved fruitless. There was evidence in the slave quarters that there had been female slaves living at the plantation, but none were found. No other slaves or casualties were found during the search.

General Sherman was summoned due to the fact that he had purposely saved this plantation. The General arrived shortly thereafter. General Johnston, of the Confederate Army, also arrived. The two generals buried the owners together in front of the house. The slaves were buried behind the house in unmarked graves. This report was made by Captain John West of the United States Army, witnessed by Judge Rodger Naugle, recorded by Nancy Plum, court secretary.

The suspects in this case are a group of men known as "bummers". This group of renegade A.W.O.L. union soldiers is suspected to be headed up by Thomas Stringer and James Carter. A search for all these men is already under way as this is not their first military crime."

Mark stood up and said, "That's all it says."
Alex rubbed his chin, "Well, at least I know more than I did when I came in here."
Mark started folding the document back to its original shape, and asked, "What else did you want to know?"
Alex studied Mark's face a moment then asked, "Did you ever experience anything strange while you were at the Wells house?"

Clarsville, Tennessee

Eddie and the girls spent the next few days packing. By Thursday afternoon, almost everything, except the clothes they were wearing, was packed in boxes and ready for the movers in the morning. "Did we forget anything?" asked Eddie.

"I don't think so," Karen responded as she thought through everything they had packed.

"Oh hell," Eddie cursed. "I almost forgot. I would never forgive myself if I left those behind. I'll be right back."

Eddie headed up the stairs to the second floor. Karen could hear the door to the attic in the ceiling being lowered. Eddie unfolded the steps and climbed up. He blindly reached for the string he knew was there that would turn on the naked bulb that hung from the rafters. He found the string and pulled, and the small area of the vast attic was lit.

Eddie sat down on the plywood he had placed up here. In front of him sat an old cigar box and two cardboard beer cases. He took the cigar box and placed it on his lap. He carefully opened the box and looked inside. He reached in and picked up a couple pieces of Confederate currency. The paper was dirty and brittle. He didn't know where his grandfather had gotten it, but he carefully returned the currency to the box.

Next, he withdrew a gold pocket watch. It didn't work and the minute hand was missing. The hour hand was pointing at the three. He held it in the palm of his hand and stroked the cracked glass face with his thumb. He had never understood the inscription on the face cover that read, "To my beloved husband. Love, Miriam." He had never known anyone in his family named Miriam. He had thought at one time that his father might have been married twice, but after thinking about it, he found it very unlikely. Maybe it was his grandpa who had been married twice. He didn't know anything much about his grandparents, they had died a few years before he was born. When he had the chance to ask his father, the need to know just wasn't there so he never asked. His father never volunteered any information so now the knowledge was lost. That had never bothered Eddie before, but now he was itching for information. Thoughtfully and carefully, he closed the face of the watch and returned it to the box and closed the lid. He gathered all three boxes into his arms and headed back down the folding steps.

Chapter Ten

Madison, Georgia

Mark looked at Alex in a strange way. "What do you mean anything strange?" Mark's tone was guarded.

"What I mean is, did anything happen that cannot easily be explained?" Mark hesitated before he spoke. Sometimes if you told people things that were unnatural they subconsciously thought you to be a little off. Mark didn't want that. He enjoyed being respected as the authority on local history. He didn't want to do anything to ruin that reputation. After having thought about it for a moment, he decided that Alex was asking a genuine question and could be trusted to keep this information to himself.

"Between you and me, I have noticed several strange things in and around the house."

"Like what?"

"This is just between us, okay?" Alex shrugged, "Sure okay."

"I worked out of that house for twelve years. In those twelve years, I have seen tables move on their own, candles light by themselves, windows open by themselves, and felt a presence with me at times. I have also seen ghosts walking up and down the main staircase. One time I was working late by myself and heard the smoke alarm going off downstairs. I went down to see what was going on. When I got to the first floor, I noticed smoke coming out of the old dining room. I ran to the kitchen to get the fire extinguisher. While I was in the kitchen, the faucet started running then shut off by itself. While I was startled at this, I was focused on putting the fire out. I turned with the extinguisher in hand and rushed back to the dining room. When I got there, the smoke was gone. I looked in every corner of the room trying to find the source of the smoke. I couldn't find a thing. The more I thought about it, I came to the conclusion that it must have had something to do with the burn spot in the middle of the floor."

Alex looked at Mark with surprise. "So there had been something burning?"

Mark raised his hand. "I didn't say that."

"Then what are you saying?"

Mark laced his fingers together and rested his hands on the table. "What I'm saying is, there has always been a burn spot on the floor. Remember the report that I read to you? It said that a slave's body had been found burned on the floor of the dining room."

"Oh yeah, that's right. I forgot about that."

"We replaced the boards on the floor twice. Each time, within a week, the burn spot returned. Finally, we left the floor alone and covered the spot with a rug. It's still there as far as I know."

Alex was quiet for a moment, scratching thoughtfully at his goatee. "Have you ever experienced anything hostile?"

"No never. What kind of hostile are you asking about?"

Alex recounted in detail what had happened to him in the cemetery. By the time Alex finished telling his story, he was visibly shaken. "What does that mean?" asked Alex.

"Well, I'm by far no parapsychologist, but I'd say the spirits don't like you very much." Mark answered with a chuckle. Alex looked both embarrassed and annoyed.

"Thanks a lot Mark. I figured that one out on my own."

"I'm sorry. I'm not making fun of you on purpose. I know this is a sensitive subject for you."

Alex composed himself and asked, "Really, why would the ghosts be aggressive toward me and not you?"

Mark looked around the room as if someone might over hear him. "You know April dabbles in that sort of thing. She might be able to give you some insight into what's going on out there."

Alex leaned back in his chair and sighed heavily. "Yeh, I know. Okay. Maybe I'll talk to her and see what she says."

As Alex got out of his chair, and pushed it back under the table, Mark said, as if reading Alex's thoughts, "I trust April completely. She's a good girl. She's very discreet if she's anything at all."

With an effort at a smile, Alex said, "I know. Thanks again Mark." As Alex made his way to the front door, he thought to himself, *At least I know I'm not going crazy. I'm not the only one who has seen things out there.*

Clarsville, Tennessee

At 7:00 a.m. on Friday morning, the movers arrived. Eddie and Karen were in the kitchen leaning on the bar drinking their coffee amid a sea of boxes. Neither had slept well in anticipation of the move. Eddie had let the movers in to start loading the truck. Morgan had gotten up with Eddie and Karen. She was at her last day of school. While she was excited about moving to Georgia, she didn't want to leave her friends behind. The excitement must have won her over because she didn't cry about it at all last night when Karen talked to her about it. Karen was so proud of Morgan. At eight years old, she was handling things like a grown up already. By 7:00 that evening, all but the beds were loaded up on the truck. Plans were that they would leave first thing in the morning. Both Karen and Eddie slept hard that night. The exertion of lifting and carrying all those boxes had worn both of them out. At dawn Eddie jumped awake. He was sweating and shaking.

Vengeful Spirits

The shadowy memories of the nightmare that shook him floated through his mind.

He was in an old house. It was dark and quiet. It looked a lot like the house they were moving to. The next thing he remembered he was outside standing in the grass. He was watching a black man sitting on top of another man. The black man was punching and clawing at the man on the ground. All of the sudden, there was a loud boom and a bright flash of light. The black man fell over with part of his head missing. The last thing he remembered was the sneering grin of a man holding a smoking shotgun.

As Eddie sat up in bed, trying to calm himself, the question kept going through his mind, *Where did that come from?*

Madison, Georgia

Alex walked into the Phoenix and went directly over to April where she was washing the beer mugs from the night before. As April looked up, she asked, "Is everything okay, Alex? We don't open 'til eleven."

Alex looked around. He was happy to see they were the only ones in the bar. "Yeah, everything's okay. I wanted to talk to ya."

"Okay, 'bout what?"

Alex steeled himself before he spoke. "You know 'bout the supernatural, right?"

Being modest, April said, "Yeah, I know a little. Why do you ask?"

"I gotta question. If a place is haunted, why would the ghosts be passive toward one person and aggressive toward another?"

April folded her dishrag, turned off the water, and leaned on the bar. She drummed her fingers on the lacquered surface as she thought. The silence was complete except for the dripping of the water in the sink. April drew in a deep breath and said, "It could be that one of them has a negative connection to the place. Are you asking about a specific place, or just in general?"

Alex wasn't expecting to have to place himself in the middle of the example. He remembered what Mark had said. *"She's discreet."* Alex looked at April's concerned eyes and figured what the hell. "This is between you and me, okay?"

April nodded without speaking.

"A couple of days ago I went to the Confederate cemetery at the Wells place." Alex retold the story to her as he had told Mark. When he was finished, he said, "Mark said that he had experienced things, but nothing aggressive the whole time he worked there. I'm there for thirty minutes, and I got attacked. I don't get it."

April thought a moment as she stared at the bar. "You say you never had any extensive interaction with the Wells place at all?"

"No. Never."

April straightened up and asked with her eyes bulging, "You didn't step on any graves, did you?"

"No. I made a point not to."

"Hmmm." April settled back onto the bar. "It's a far stretch, but it's possible that one of your ancestors

Vengeful Spirits

had a violent connection with the house. It's called a generational curse."

Alex could feel the knot tightening in his stomach again, as a feeling of dread oozed over him. "I could go by the place and see if I pick up any vibrations. Sometimes that one thing can tell you a lot."

Alex stood up and put his hat on hoping she couldn't see the fear and dread he felt inside. "Thanks baby. I'll letcha know." Alex walked to his car with his keys in hand. *What if this Edward Stringer is related to Thomas Stringer? He will be putting a fuse in a powder keg and won't even know it.*

Saturday morning Alex woke at dawn with a start. He was short of breath and sweating. At first he thought he was having an asthma attack. He swung his feet out of bed and sat with his face in his hands. Slowly he began to remember the dream he had that had startled him awake. He was at the Wells plantation behind the house. He remembered he was carrying a shotgun. It was dark outside and he was pushing and yelling at slaves. Another man came walking across the yard pushing a young female slave in front of him. In a flash, a large black man jumped on top of him and started punching him. In the dream, he stepped up and pointed the shotgun at the black man's head and pulled the trigger. The night exploded with a flash and a boom. The black man slumped over with the top of his head missing. The last thing he remembered is waking up and struggling to breathe.

Clarsville, Tennessee

The movement in the bed woke Karen. Sleepily, she asked Eddie, "You okay, dear?" without turning over. When Eddie didn't answer she turned over and saw Eddie's white face and sweaty body. Instantly she was awake. "Eddie! Are you okay?" she asked, as she shook his arm. Eddie stared blankly at the wall without answering her.

Karen shook him a second time and Eddie responded, "Huh? What? Did you say something?"

"Eddie, are you okay? You're white as a sheet and you're soaking wet."

Karen put her hand on Eddie's forehead. "Are you sick?"

Eddie shook his head, "No. I just had a bad dream, that's all."

"A bad dream? You look like you've lived through a nightmare."

"I'll be okay. I just need a shower. I'm sure I'll be fine once I'm all cleaned up."

Eddie kissed Karen on the cheek and said, "Thanks for taking care of me sweetheart. I'm going to get a shower."

Karen watched as Eddie walked across the room to the shower. She noticed that his t-shirt was stuck to his back from all the sweat. She waited until he was in the shower before she got out of bed to wake Morgan.

By 7:30, the movers had returned and had started packing the last of the items into the moving truck. By

9:00, Eddie, Karen, and Morgan were leading the way out of town toward Georgia with the moving truck in tow. Beside Eddie on the front seat was the cigar box with the lid taped closed. The other two boxes were in the trunk.

Ever since Eddie held that pocket watch in his hand in the attic he had the strongest feeling that it was something very important. He didn't know of what significance it was but until he found out he wasn't going to let it out of his sight.

Chapter Eleven

Madison, Georgia

Alex stood up from the bed and scratched his butt through his briefs and looked out the window. The trees in the backyard cast long black shadows across the backyard toward the house like black ink inching its way toward him. The rising sun painted the sky orange, red, and purple. It looked like a pretty day ahead. No matter how pretty the sky was the feeling of urgency and dread continued to eat away at him.

After a shower, Alex got a cup of coffee and grabbed the paper off the front lawn. He needed to call April. He had to find out as much as he could about the Wells house. He picked up the phone and dialed. He knew it was early to be calling April, but he wanted to get started on things as soon as he could and April was the first source of information that he knew of. After four rings, April answered. He could tell she was still asleep, but he pressed on.

"Hey baby, it's me." Immediately she was wide awake.

"What's wrong? What happened?" Alex was surprised at how she reacted. He was hoping to hear her sleepy voice whisper over the phone, "Hey sweetie".

"Hey, hey, calm down. Everything is okay. I'm calling on a personal matter, not a police matter." Alex could hear her let out the breath she had been holding.

"Oh good. You scared me a minute. I thought somethin' had happened."

"I want to take you up on your offer to check out the Wells place."

"Really? I didn't think your curiosity would get the best of you."

"Well, it did. What time can you be out there?"

"Ummm, what time is it now?"

Alex looked at the clock on the oven, "it's 7:30 now."

"How's 9:00 sound?"

"Great. I'll call Alice at the office and tell her I need the key to the house for police business. I'll get the key, and meet you out there. Okay?"

"Okay. I'll see you at nine."

April arrived at the Wells place at nine, but Alex wasn't there yet. She stepped out of her '63 Chevy II, and stared at the house. She looked around at the surrounding landscape. She had been here before, but not to "feel for spirits". She could see the Wells headstones through the fence that surrounded their resting places. In the distance, she could see the Confederate cemetery. "Well I might as well start lookin' around." She closed the door to her car and headed toward the cemetery.

She remembered the story Alex had told her about his experience in the cemetery. Though she knew things like that were possible, she continued on without fear.

She stood between the two pillars flanking the entrance. She held out her hands and extended her arms. She closed her eyes and took a few steps into the cemetery. Immediately she could smell smoke from a campfire, and the faint smell of cooking stew. She could hear the sound of men talking and laughing. She also heard what sounded like a banjo playing and men singing.

She opened her eyes and saw misty, faint apparitions of soldiers sitting around campfires as if the cemetery wasn't even there. She stood in the middle of the vision from the past and stared in disbelief. Out of the corner of her eye, she saw a man approaching her. He had taken his hat off, and walked slowly toward her. April had to forcefully keep herself from running out of the cemetery. She didn't feel threatened, she actually felt safe. This was a new experience for her. The only thing she'd ever experienced before was the presence of a spirit. She had never "seen" the presence of a spirit. It wasn't the sort of thing she saw on a daily basis so she was a bit jumpy.

The man stood in front of her smiling. He had an unkempt beard, shoes with holes in them, and filthy clothes that looked like they were stained with Georgia clay. She could also smell the fact that he hadn't bathed in a while. The man extended his hand and took her hand in his. The touch was warm, like holding a warm cup of tea. "Don't be afraid. I want to introduce myself. I am your grandfather Phillip. I know you have seen me before. Not in person, but from the pictures at your parent's house."

Then it struck her. That's where she remembered this man from. She remembered her father telling her about granddaddy Phil when he would show her pictures.

Suddenly the hand grew colder. The atmosphere had changed. She couldn't hear the music or the men's voices anymore. The smells changed to gun smoke and rotting flesh. Her grandfather said, as he began to fade away, "Someone is coming." The air had become chilly and a breeze began to blow. The apparition that had moments ago seemed like a friendly long lost relative now appeared to be a dangerous and angry force to be reckoned with. She gathered her courage as she quickly exited the cemetery. As she passed the pillars at the entrance, it was like stepping out of a freezer. As she turned to look back at the cemetery, she heard the crunch of gravel and saw Alex pull up to the house.

Vengeful Spirits

Alex waited by his car. After his experience the last time he was here, he wasn't going anywhere near the cemetery.

As April approached Alex's car, he said, "Sorry I'm late. I had a time gettin' the key from Alice. Did you check out the cemetery?"

"Yeah, I figured I would look around outside 'til you got here."

"Well? Did you notice anything? Did you pick up any vibes? What happened?"

April told Alex what she experienced while Alex listened intently. "Then as soon as you pulled into the driveway, things….. changed."

"Holy shit! You actually saw ghosts? That's so awe…..wait a minute. You said when I got here things changed? What do you mean changed? How did they change?"

April had a stressed sympathetic look on her face. "Well, at first the atmosphere was light and friendly. It had a warm, inviting feel to it. When you got here, the feelin' changed drastically, and so did my grandfather and the other ghosts. The atmosphere felt aggressive and tense. It was like flippin' a switch. All of the sudden the air got bitter cold. It felt like I was standin' in a barren wasteland. The vibes from the ghosts changed also. They suddenly were filled with rage, hatred, and bitterness. Before my grandfather's ghost disappeared, he told me that someone was comin'. He didn't sound very happy about it either."

After a moment, April asked, "Are you sure you haven't spent any time here before?"

Alex was in another world. Finally April touched his arm and shook him.

Alex snapped to and said, "Huh? What? I'm sorry. What did you say?"

With an exasperated sigh, April asked again, "Are you sure you haven't been here before because you definitely have an affect on this place."

"Yeah, I'm sure."

April studied his face for a moment. Alex looked at her in return and said, "I swear I haven't. Other than patrols, I've never been down here."

April smiled, "Okay. Alright, I believe you. Where's the key to the house? I want to look around inside."

"I've got it right here in my coat pocket." Alex reached in his pocket and said, "What the hell?" It looked to April that the key was stuck in his pocket. Alex tried to pull the key out, but it wouldn't budge.

"What's wrong?" asked April.

"The key, it's ice cold. I think it's frozen to the inside of my pocket."

"Aw, c'mon Alex, just give me the key."

"I'm serious. Feel my fingers." Alex removed his hand and April felt his fingers. They were ice cold and had a blue tint to them.

"Oh, my God," exclaimed April. "Here let me try." April stuck her hand in his pocket and felt the key. She expected to feel the sting of the frozen key. Instead, she touched the keys and they were warm. She pulled the keys out of his pocket and stared at them. Alex was cupping his hands to his mouth and blowing into them to warm them up. When April pulled the keys out and held them in her hand, Alex looked shocked.

"Hey! How did you do that?" Alex reached out to grab the keys then stopped his hand in midair and thought better of it.

"Maybe it would be better if I went into the house myself first."

Alex looked at the keys then his hand. "Yeah, that might be a good idea."

April turned and started toward the house. When she got to the front porch, she stopped and looked to her right on the floor. To Alex it looked like she was looking at something in front of the rocking chairs. She drew her attention away from the porch and looked about halfway up the wall to the Widow's Walk. Quickly she turned and looked at Alex. Her face was pale and she looked nervous. "Stay there. I'll be back in a few minutes." She turned, unlocked the door, and disappeared into the house.

Chapter Twelve

Dalton, Georgia

Around noon Eddie, the girls, and the moving truck stopped in Dalton, Georgia for lunch. As they pulled into the McDonald's, Eddie said to Karen, "You two go on inside and order. I've got to make reservations for all of us at the motel in Madison for tonight. I forgot to call before we left."

As the Impala came to a stop in the parking lot, Karen said, "Okay. You want your usual?"

Eddie smiled, "Yeah, the usual."

Karen and Morgan got out and headed toward the front door. Eddie stepped out of the car and made it over to the lone pay phone.

Just as he put his hand on the phone the moving truck driver walked up and asked, "Mr. Stringer, you did save us a room in Madison, didn't you?"

Eddie smiled sheepishly, "I was just going to do that. It slipped my mind this morning. Don't worry. We'll all have a place to sack out tonight."

The driver smiled, "Great. Thanks Mr. Stringer."

The driver walked away to join the three other movers waiting for him in the middle of the parking lot. The driver gave them the thumbs up, and the four of them walked into the McDonald's.

Eddie pulled out the pamphlet from the motel that he kept from last weekend. He dialed the number and waited. A familiar man's voice answered, "Madison Manor."

Eddie responded, "Yes, my name is Edward Stringer. I need to reserve three rooms for tonight and tomorrow night."

The voice sounded excited, "Mr. Stringer. How nice to hear from you again. You were with us last weekend, weren't you? Just can't get enough of our little town, huh?"

"Well, actually, I'm moving to your little town. I've bought the Wells mansion. My family and the movers need a place to stay until we get moved in."

"Congratulations! You liked our town so much you decided to move in. That's great."

"Yes, I'll be working with Louis Ormand at his law office on the square."

"Well, let me be the first to welcome you to Madison as a new resident. I have three rooms reserved for you. I'll have the keys waiting for you at the desk. See you when you get here, Mr. Stringer."

"Thank you. I should be there late this afternoon." Eddie hung up the phone. With a sigh, he said to himself, "Okay, let's eat." As Eddie walked by the car, he reached inside and covered the cigar box with a blanket and locked the doors.

Madison, Georgia

April stood in the breezeway at the front door. She stood feeling the vibrations of the house. The house seemed to wrap its arms around her. She felt like she had come home. She walked into the parlor on her right. The only actual furniture in the room was a mirror hanging from the wall. The rest of the room was barren over the wood paneled floor. As she looked in the room an apparition of two men and a woman sitting on what looked like cots appeared before her eyes. They were talking to each other. One of the men looked like a Confederate general. The general looked sad and distressed. April's heart went out to the apparition. Slowly the image began to fade. Within minutes, the apparition was gone and the room was empty again.

She left the parlor and went down the hall to the dining room. She sat down on the antique sofa, and closed her eyes. Immediately, she smelled smoke. It didn't smell like smoke that would be coming from the fireplace against the facing wall. It smelled like.... burning hair and flesh. She opened her eyes, and saw the shadowy form of a man lying on the floor. The man was on fire, but he wasn't moving. His head had a strange shape to it. She watched in fascination as the ghostly flames licked up into the air. Suddenly, she could hear footsteps. She couldn't tell where they were coming from, but she could hear them over the crackling and hissing of the fire. At the blink of an eye, the man jumped up and headed for the door screaming. When April looked toward the door, she saw Alex leaning on the door frame watching her like nothing was happening. April screamed, "Alex, look out!!" Alex turned around and looked behind him. As soon as the burning ghost reached Alex at the doorway, it disappeared. Alex spun back around as the ghost disappeared into nothingness.

He looked at April and asked tensely, "Hey, what's wrong? And what's that smell?"
April looked at Alex with horror and disbelief.
"What are you doing in here? I told you to wait outside."
"I got bored. What's that burnt smell?" Alex sniffed the air then sniffed his shirt. "Aw, man, this stinks. Were you burnin' somethin' in here? My shirt smells like burnt flesh." April stood up, and headed for the front door. As she passed Alex, she grabbed his arm and pulled him along with her. Once they were outside, on the front porch, April locked the door and headed for her car. Alex followed.
"What's goin' on? What happened in there?"

April stopped at her car and leaned on the fender. "You remember when I told you you have an affect on this place?"

"Yeah. What kind of affect?"

"A negative affect. Like it or not, either you or someone in your family has been here before and caused a lot of pain and sufferin'. You need to find out what it is soon. With you in that house, dangerous things could happen. Find out what happened at this house in relation to your family in the past. Then, find a way to make amends."

April tossed the keys to Alex. He dodged them like they were a live hand grenade. They landed at his feet. Slowly Alex bent down. With one finger, he touched the keys.

"Hey, they're not cold anymore." Carefully Alex picked up the keys and put them back in his pocket.

April got in her car and started it up. She rolled down the driver's side window and said to Alex, "Come by the bar when you get finished with your runnin' 'round and we'll talk some more." Alex stuck his head in the window and gave her a kiss.

"I'll be by later. Maybe we'll eat lunch." Alex stood and watched as April's car disappeared toward town.

Alex stood staring at the house. For the second time Alex said to his grandfather as if he were standing right next to him, "Grandpa, what the hell happened here? What did you do?" Alex turned away from the house and started to get into his car. He noticed the two graves under the magnolia tree. He had seen them before, but never stopped to read the plaque that stood behind them. He walked over and stood in front of the graves and read the plaque. "Josiah and Miriam Wells." *Why do I feel there's some sort of connection here? Like I should know who these people are.* The realization hit him like a runaway freight train. "Miriam Wells. M.W. That's the monogram on the platter that I have at home in the basement." Quickly, the wind picked up. He heard a voice in the wind that whispered angrily in his ear. "THIEF!" With the speed of a jackrabbit, he returned to the safety of his car.

The wind had died as quickly has it had come. Alex sat in his car, and hit the steering wheel in frustration. "Damn! Every time I come out here and I'm by myself shit happens." Alex sat trying to calm himself for a few moments. Suddenly, Alex realized where the platter came from. "Grandpa stole it from Mrs. Wells. Grandpa was here at this house. Damn it, Grandpa! Why couldn't you leave well enough alone?" Alex started the car, and headed straight for home. He was now on the right track to making amends with his past.

Chapter Thirteen

Madison Manor Hotel

At 5:15, Eddie and the movers parked in the parking lot of the Madison Manor Hotel. Everybody waited outside while Eddie went to the office to retrieve the room keys. Apparently Eddie's arrival was common knowledge because as soon as he opened the door the manager from behind the counter, who he didn't recognize, said, "Mr. Stringer, glad to see you had a safe trip. We have your rooms ready for you."

Surprised at the recognition, he stuttered a second and said, "Uh…….yes. We had a safe trip. It was long, but safe."

"If you'll just sign the register you can go straight up to your rooms. On a chilly evening like this I'm sure y'all will enjoy a hot shower and some t.v. We also have room service if you and your family are too tired to go out."

Eddie noticed the girl standing behind the manager. She was holding her hands in front of her and smiled politely when she and Eddie made eye contact. Eddie felt a little uneasy with the way she was staring at him, but he let it slide.

After Eddie signed in, he told the manager, "Thanks, a hot shower and room service sounds good right now."

The manager smiled, "Here are your keys. All of the rooms are next to each other. Enjoy your stay. If you need anything, don't hesitate to call me and ask."

Eddie took the keys and responded, "Thanks again. See ya later."

Eddie walked over to the movers standing by their truck. He handed the driver two keys. "I got you and the guys two rooms to split. Is that okay?"

The four men smiled past their tired eyes, "Thanks Mr. Stringer. That'll be great. What time do we need to get going in the morning?"

Eddie thought a minute then said, "I guess we can sleep in a little in the morning. Let's say 8:30. They have a continental breakfast in the lobby at 7:00 if y'all want something before we get started. I'm planning to get a bite myself before we leave."

The driver nodded, "Okay Mr. Stringer. We'll be waiting by the truck at 8:30. See y'all in the mornin'."

Eddie and Karen both said in unison, "Good night."

In the office the girl behind the counter was looking at Eddie's signature and asking the manager, "Do you think he's related? The last name is the same."

The manager was somewhat edgy about the subject. "I don't know. If he is we can't blame him for what his ancestors did. He hadn't even been born yet. Whatever your feelings are, I expect you to act professional around him and all our guests. Understand?"

The girl nodded her head and said, "Yes sir." The manager then disappeared into his office and settled behind his desk. The girl remained at the counter rubbing her finger over Eddie's signature remembering what she had learned in her local history class in school last semester.

Two men named Thomas Stringer and James Carter were the only two men never caught for the lynching and murders at the Wells Plantation in 1865. She knew that the deputy's name was Carter, but he had been around for so long and Carter was such a common name, she didn't give him much thought. After hearing the rumor that a man named Stringer was buying the Wells place, she started to get suspicious. *Maybe he doesn't even know about the lynchings or his family history. Maybe he's not even related.* She didn't know if ghosts were real or not, but she had heard the stories about the happenings at the house and told herself if the ghosts are real, they'll know.

621 Hill Street

Alex sat in his basement at his workbench with the serving platter on his lap. He sat with his eyes closed, his hands resting on the platter. He was recalling all of the information he had gathered on the Wells place. He remembered what Mark had read to him from the report filed the day of the discovery. Suddenly as if he'd gotten shocked, he opened his eyes and snapped his head up. "That's what seemed odd. All of the slaves accounted for were male. No female slaves were ever found. I wonder why. The bandits surely didn't take 'em when they left. What happened to 'em?"

Alex looked at his watch. It was only 5:30. Alex had Mark's home number upstairs in his rolodex. Alex hopped off the stool and left the platter on the work bench.

He sat in his office and dialed Mark's number. After two rings, Mark picked up.

"Hello?"

Alex couldn't hide his excitement. "Mark, it's Alex."

"Hey Al. What's up? You sound a little excited. Is everything okay?"

"Yeah, everything's okay. Remember when you read that report to me?"

"Yeah?"

"The report stated that the slaves found on the front steps were all male. Right?"

"Yeah, I believe so. Why? What are you getting at?"

"Where were the female slaves?"

The line was silent. "Mark, are you there?"

After a moment, Mark replied, "Yeah, I'm here."

"Well…….what do you think happened to 'em? Is it likely Josiah only had male slaves?"

"No. I know he had at least one female slave. I think her name was Fannie or something like that. All slave owners had to have an inventory of their slaves. I know that I don't have copies of those at the society. Maybe the Georgia archives in Atlanta does. I'll call first thing Monday morning and check."

"Okay. Let me know first thing when you find out somethin'. Okay?"

"Alright. I'll get in touch with you Monday sometime."

"Thanks Mark."

As Alex hung up the phone, he felt like he was looking for something he really didn't want to know, but curiosity wouldn't let him go. Alex ran down to the basement and put the platter in a paper sack. He stuck the sack under his arm and headed up the stairs and toward the front door.

The Phoenix

Alex pulled into the parking lot at the Phoenix. It was cold and windy. He had to park in the back parking lot. It was Saturday night and the place was hoppin'.

Before getting out of his car, he zipped up his coat. It wasn't much, but it was better than nothing. Alex grabbed the paper sack off the front seat and headed toward the front door. The wind was blowing leaves and trash across the lot. Alex hurried his progress. The chill of the steady wind cut through his jacket like the jab of an ice pick. The cold went straight to the bone. When he got to the front door, he hurried in and pulled it closed against the wind behind him.

The music was loud, along with the noise of people talking and laughing. The cloud of smoke that filled the room was so thick that if you didn't smoke, you did if you were in the room. The pool tables were full, along with the dart boards.

Alex looked over at the bar, "Where's April?" he asked the barkeep. The man pointed to the booth at the end of the bar. April sat sipping a cup of coffee and eating a cookie. *She must be on her break.* Quickly, Alex pushed his way through the cluster of patrons and sat on the other side of the booth from April.

Startled, April spoke around a mouthful of cookie, "Al! What are you doing here?" As focused as Alex was on his reason for being here he had to laugh. The combination of the look on April's face and the fact that she spewed cookie crumbs all over the table when she spoke was just completely hilarious and sexy at the same time. Once Alex quit laughing, and April swallowed what was left of the cookie that was in her mouth, she asked, "What's up?" as she eyed the bag.

Madison Manor Hotel

Eddie and the girls had packed suitcases with enough clothes and essentials for three days. Karen had thought ahead and knew it would take at least a day or more to even find their clothes after they moved in. There must have been a hundred boxes that looked alike. She kicked herself for not labeling them while she was packing.

Eddie had brought the luggage to the room and sat it on the bed. Karen was taking a shower and Morgan was watching t.v. As Eddie lay down on the bed, a thought struck him. *I should bring in the cigar box from the car. What if it gets stolen?* He sat up on the bed and looked at Morgan. She was absorbed in Dragnet. He stood and reached in his pocket for his keys. They weren't there. He looked around the room, "Mo, have you seen daddy's keys?"

Without looking away from the t.v. she shook her head and said, "Uh, uh." He took a few steps toward the door and spotted them on the table by the window. When he reached down to grab the keys, he noticed the gold pocket watch sitting next to them. Eddie froze. He acted like the watch was a coiled snake ready to strike. He pulled his hand back and away from the watch.

He turned to Morgan again. She was still watching t.v., "Punkin' did your mommy bring in the cigar box that was on the front seat?" This time she looked at him.

"Nope. It was there when I got out of the car."

Eddie went to the bathroom door and knocked.

"Yeah?" the reply came.

"Hey Kar, did you grab the cigar box off the front seat?"

"No, I thought if you wanted it, you'd get it."

"Okay, I'm going to the car to get it."

"Okay, you can have the shower when you get back. I'm almost done."

Eddie closed the door. *I must have brought the watch in without thinking about it. Well, I'll go get the box from the car anyway.*

Eddie went to the table to get his keys. *The watch! It's gone!* Eddie once again turned to Morgan, "Sweetie, did you grab the pocket watch off the table?"

Morgan was still on the bed, watching t.v. "What pocket watch?"

"Never mind." *Maybe it's just stress, but I swear I saw the watch on the table just a second ago. I'll check the car. If the watch is there, then maybe I'm just stressed out.*

Eddie got to the car and grabbed the box off the front seat. He slammed the door and locked it. He sat the box on the hood of the car. The tape he used to keep the lid closed was still attached. He pulled the tape loose and opened the box. The watch was there, but something else was missing. He stood staring into the box trying to figure out what was missing. Then it struck him. The money. The Confederate paper bills that had covered the bottom of the box were now gone. *What the hell is going on here? Is someone playing games with me?* He slammed the top closed and replaced the tape. Quickly he walked across the parking lot and returned to his room.

Karen was drying her hair in front of the mirror when Eddie opened the door. She looked at his reflection and turned to face him. "Eddie, what's wrong?"

"Something's missing."

Karen reached behind her on the counter and picked something up. She turned back to Eddie. "By the way, are these yours? I found them by the sink when I got out of the shower." Karen was holding a stack of Confederate bills in her hand.

"Eddie, what's wrong? You look like you've seen a ghost."

Chapter Fourteen

The Phoenix

Alex eyed April with a serious stare. "I've got somethin' in this bag I want you to……..touch. I want you to tell me if you get a feelin' from it."

April sighed. "Alex, I don't do parlor tricks. I take my gift very seriously."

"I know. That's why I'm here. I have a suspicion about the object in the bag, and I want you to confirm or deny my suspicions."

"Are you goin' to let me see what's in the bag?"

"No. I want your impressions just from what you feel and that's all."

April held out her hands on the table. "Okay. Slide me the bag."

Alex slid the bag across the table in front of April. She slid her petite hands into the bag. She closed her eyes and tilted her head back. Alex enjoyed the warm flush from what he was thinking. *My God, she is sexy. I would love to......* Alex's thoughts were brought to a screeching halt as April took a panicked, fearful breath. She opened her eyes and pulled her trembling hands out of the bag.

"April, are you okay? What's wrong?" April looked at Alex with haunted eyes and a pale face.

"This doesn't belong to you. The person it belonged to was lynched and decapitated. Her spirit wants it back. Where did you get this?"

Alex looked away in shame.

At that moment, April's eyes and voice changed. Her jade eyes changed to burning red and her soft voice turned raspy and dry. Like the strike of a serpent, April's hand quickly clamped Alex's arm like a vice and jerked him up onto the top of the table until they were eye to eye. Her eyes were filled with hate and her voice was cold.

"I want what's mine, you filthy yankee bastard." An instant later, April's grip loosened and her eyes were normal again. She looked like she had just woken up. She was as limp as a dishrag as she slumped on the table. The event only took seconds and Alex was still trying to figure out if what happened had actually happened.

Alex reached over and touched her shoulder. "April, you okay?"

April raised her head off the table and stared at Alex bleary-eyed. Her forehead was damp from sweat. "What just happened?"

Madison Manor Hotel

Eddie looked at Karen sternly and asked, "Did you get those out of this box?"

Karen was shaken by his question and his tone. "No, I never touched the box. What is this and why do you have it?" Karen was waving the bills around toward Eddie.

Eddie sat on the bed. He could tell she was as confused as he was. "It's Confederate money. I'm not sure where it originally came from, but it was in this box with some other stuff my dad had saved over the years." Eddie told her about the pocket watch and then about the money. When Eddie finished talking, she came over and sat with him on the bed. Morgan was still on the other bed watching t.v., not paying them any attention. Karen handed him the money and Eddie put it back in the box. He was happy to see that the pocket watch was still there.

Karen put her arm around him and reminded him, "We've been under a lot of stress lately. Please don't let the little things bother you so much."

Eddie looked at Karen and smiled. He had really let his imagination get the best of him. Maybe he just needed a good nights rest.

"Okay baby. I'm sorry. I guess I'm just a bit wound up. I'm going to take a hot shower then we can order some room service. How's that sound?"

"Room service?" Morgan finally piped in.

"Yeah, that sound good to you, punkin'?"

"Yeah, I'm starved."

Eddie sat the box on the table and grabbed the menu. "You girls decide what y'all want to eat while I'm in the shower." As Eddie headed toward the bathroom, he took one last look at the box on the table. It was right where he left it. *Good. Now just stay there and don't move.* He thought to himself as he closed the bathroom door and began to undress.

The Phoenix

Alex looked at April and said, "Ewww, you don't look so good."

"I don't feel so good. I feel like I've been put through the wringer."

The barkeep saw April and came over with a glass of water. "You gonna be alright darlin'?"

"I hope so," April answered as she took a long gulp of the cold ice water. "I think I'm gonna hafta call it quits for the night."

The barkeep nodded his approval. "I think that might be a good idea. You look like you could use some rest."

Alex looked at the barkeep. "I'll drive her home."

"Okay Alex. Thanks. Take good care of her."

He looked at April and said, "Don't worry about this place. I can handle it." The barkeep slapped Alex's back and returned to the bar.

"You ready to go?" asked Alex.

With great effort, April managed, "Yeah, let's go."

Alex pulled into April's driveway. He got out and went around to April's door to help her out. When he opened the door, she practically fell out onto the ground. Alex put his arms under her and carried her to the porch door. While Alex was holding her, April fished her keys out and unlocked the door.

Alex carried her to the bedroom and laid her on the bed. He pulled her boots off then pulled her jeans and top off. Next, he reached into the dresser drawer and pulled out her nightshirt. He sat her up in the bed and pulled the nightshirt over her head.

He reached down and pulled the covers up over her and said, "You gonna be alright by yourself or do you want me to stay with you tonight?" April lay on her back not responding. Before turning off the light, he bent down and kissed her gently on the lips. Still she didn't respond. He reached over and brushed her hair away from her face. Gently he bent down and whispered in her ear, "G'night baby. I love you. I'll call ya in the mornin'." He switched the light off, and locked the door on his way out.

621 Hill Street

Alex got home to a ringing phone. He quickly unlocked the door and rushed inside to answer it. Three quick steps across the kitchen got him to the phone. He snagged the receiver off the hook, "Hello?"

"Deputy Carter? This is Charlene at dispatch."

"Hey Charlene. What's goin' on? Is everything okay?"

"Yeah, sure, Alex. Everything's fine. I took a message for you earlier and thought it might be important."

"Who was it that called?"

"Uhhh, it was a sheriff from Clarsville, Tennessee."

"What did he want?"

"He didn't say. He just left his name and number and wanted you to call him back at your earliest convenience."

"Okay. Let me have his name and number and I'll give him a call. What time did he call?"

"It was about an hour ago so I guess it was about 9:00."

"Alright, thanks Charlene. I appreciate it. I'll see ya in the mornin'."

"Sure thing Alex. See ya tomorrow."

As soon as Alex hung up the phone with Charlene, he dialed the number that Charlene had given him. One question rolled over in his mind. *Why is a sheriff from Tennessee calling me? And what could he possibly want?*

On the third ring a man answered with a southern drawl, "Hello?"

"Is this Sheriff Crowder?"

"Yeah, who's this?"

"My name is Deputy Alex Carter from Morgan County, Georgia. I got the message that you called."

"Yeah, I did. This is a personal matter, so just call me Rich."

"Okay, Rich. You said this is a personal matter?"

"Yeah, there's a man movin' to your town named Edward Stringer. I think he's buyin' an old plantation house."

Once again at the mention of Stringer's name, Alex got edgy and nervous. "Yeah, I've heard that rumor around town. I haven't met him yet, but I guess I will soon enough."

"You need to go and introduce yourself, and help him out in any way you can."

Alex was suddenly confused. "Why? Is he a witness or a narc?"

"No! Absolutely not! He's one of us."

Alex was still confused so he continued his line of questioning. "He's a lawman?"

With frustration in his voice, Richard said, "No. He's a loyal member of our Invisible Empire."

The line was silent a moment. Alex thought to himself, *this is just what I need to have an excuse to talk to him.*

"Alex, you still there?"

"Yeah, I'm here. I think they're movin' in tomorrow. I saw a movin' truck at the motel tonight. I'll go by the house tomorrow and check in with him."

"Good. Eddie is a very good friend of mine. Take good care of him. He's a real warrior. He's not afraid to get his hands dirty, if you know what I mean. Besides, he's your brother in the Empire."

"Don't worry Rich. He'll have a good home here. I'll keep your number on hand in case there is any problem with his membership transfer."

"Thanks Alex."

"Sure thing Rich."

As Alex hung up the phone, he knew how he was going to get the information from Eddie that he needed.

Chapter Fifteen

Madison Manor Hotel

After dinner Eddie and the girls sat on the beds watching t.v. By 10:00 Morgan was asleep. Karen pulled her clothes off and tucked her into bed. Eddie had been lying around in his boxers and t-shirt so he just pulled the sheets back and slid in.

Karen came to bed wearing her nightshirt and panties. The both of them laid there with the light on talking about tomorrow. Finally, it was time for lights out. Eddie rolled over to turn off the light. He took a last look at the cigar box on the table. The box still sat where he left it with Karen's over night bag sitting on top of it. A smile crawled across his face as he switched off the light.

Eddie awoke in complete darkness. He looked at the alarm clock on the nightstand. It read 3:01. *Why am I awake? What woke me?* He could hear the steady rhythm of Karen's breathing beside him. He could make out the lump on Morgan's bed. He laid his head back down on the pillow. As his head hit the pillow, it also hit something small and hard. He reached behind his head and grabbed the object. It was round and smooth. Just by feeling it, Eddie knew what it was. "The watch." He held the watch up to his ear. "And it's ticking."

At the Well's plantation all was quiet except for the sound of hundreds of Confederate soldiers surrounding the house. As if a page from history was being reread, the activity around the house mirrored what happened a hundred years ago. Even the smell of campfires would be noticed if there was anyone there to notice it.

Morgan County Sheriff's Department

On Sunday morning when Alex got to the sheriff's office he called April to see how she was feeling. Alex stood with the phone to his ear as he waited for her to answer.

"Hello?"

"Hey baby, it's me. How ya feelin'? How'd you sleep?"

"I feel a little rough around the edges. I guess I slept okay. I don't remember much of it because I was asleep. I do remember one thing though."

"Oh yeah? What's that?"

"The kiss."

Vengeful Spirits

Alex smiled to himself. "Yeah, what about it?"

"I thought it was sweet. I'm glad you were there to take care of me when I needed it."

"Well I'm always takin' care of everybody else. I figured it was your turn."

"I'll tell ya one thing, the fact that I won your heart makes me the luckiest man on earth. You really are the greatest April."

"Thanks baby. Look I gotta go. I'll talk to ya later, okay?"

"Alright. I'll see ya later."

As Alex hung up the phone, he realized that with April is where he wanted to be for the rest of his life.

Eddie didn't sleep the rest of the night. With confusion and annoyance, he put the watch back in the box. He sat up all night watching the box for something to happen, but nothing did.

Wells Plantation

At 9:00, when they arrived at their new house, with the movers, Eddie was already wiped out. He struggled to maintain momentum while moving around. He knew if he stopped to take a break he would go to sleep so he pushed on.

At 11:00, a police car pulled into the driveway and stopped. Karen was standing next to Eddie on the front walkway when Karen turned to Eddie and asked, "I wonder what he wants?"

Eddie shrugged his shoulders, "I don't know. Here take these boxes to the kitchen and I'll find out."

Jay Duckett

As Eddie approached the car, a deputy sheriff got out. He had dark curly hair, dark eyes, and an athletic build. As the deputy put his hat on, he looked at Eddie and asked,

"Are you Edward Stringer?" Immediately Alex saw the Klan ring on Eddie's right hand, and he knew that he had the right man.

"Yes sir, I am." Eddie extended his hand to shake Alex's. Alex returned Eddie's handshake.

"I'm Deputy Alex Carter." As Alex shook his hand, he turned Eddie's hand over to see the ring. "Nice ring."

When Eddie looked down to his hand, Alex turned his hand up to show an identical ring. Quickly Eddie's head snapped up.

Alex looked Eddie in the eyes, "Yes, I'm a member. Richard Crowder called me and told me you were movin' down this way. I just wanted you to know you have family here as well. Our family here isn't quite as big as yours back home, but we're still family."

Eddie was still in shock, "Uhhh……thanks Deputy."

"Please, call me Alex."

"Okay Deputy Alex."

Both men laughed and chatted a minute.

"Hey how 'bout you bring your family to the Phoenix for supper tonight?"

"What's the Phoenix?"

"It's the local bar and general hangout."

"Do you really think it'd be a good place for my wife and daughter?"

Vengeful Spirits

"Sure. It's Sunday night, so things'll be quiet. Besides I want y'all to meet April."

"Who's April? Your wife?"

"No." *Not yet.* "She's my girlfriend that works at the bar. How 'bout six o'clock?"

Eddie looked at his watch. "Ummm...... okay. We should be done unloading by then. Where is it?"

"It's at the corner of Washington and 441, on the square. Ya can't miss it." As Alex opened his car door he said, "See y'all at six."

Eddie waved and walked back to the moving truck to retrieve more of the seemingly endless supply of unmarked boxes.

As Eddie headed toward the front door with an arm load of boxes, he passed Karen.

"Have you seen Morgan?"

"I thought she was with you."

"She was for a little while. Now I can't find her."

"Here take these. I'll see if I can find her. She's probably scouting out her new house."

Eddie walked ahead of Karen and peeked into each first floor room off the breezeway. As he searched, he called to her, "Morgan?...... well she's not down here." Eddie went upstairs to look. "Morgan? Damn, where can she be?" Eddie finished his sweep of the upstairs at the back of the house. As he stood in the breezeway, he noticed the doors to the Widow's Walk were cracked open. "Aha! Found her. Morgan?" He got to the doors and opened them. No Morgan. He stepped out onto the walk, and leaned on the railing.

Karen called up from below, "Did you find her yet?"

"No. Not yet. I'll keep looking."

Eddie watched as Karen and the movers worked like ants gathering food for the winter. They were steadily going back and forth from the truck to the house. As he was looking down at the porch, he felt two hands shove him at the top of his back. He tightened his grip on the railing, but still almost fell over the side. Quickly he spun around to see who had pushed him. He knew it wasn't Morgan. The hands felt too big and the shove was much too strong for a little girl.

The gray shadow of a man disappeared as Eddie spun around. He caught a glimpse of it, but barely noticed it as it was gone in an instant. Regaining his balance and suppressing his instant fear, he stepped back inside and locked the doors.

As he headed back down the stairs, he remembered he hadn't checked the small rooms at the back of the house near the kitchen. He resumed his chant. "Morgan?"

He opened the door to one of the small rooms. "Morgan!" The little girl was sitting in the middle of the room with her Annie doll facing away from the door. At the sound of Eddie's voice, she turned around.

"Hi Daddy."

"Sweetie what are you doing? I've been looking all over for you."

Vengeful Spirits

Morgan smiled, "I'm playing with my new friend. Her name is Fannie. She lives here too. This is her room."

Eddie was speechless for a moment. Once his confusion cleared, he said, "Baby nobody else lives here. This is our house now."

"Yeah, but......"

"C'mon punkin', help mommy and me finish unpacking so we can go eat tonight."

Morgan stood up. "Okay." Once Morgan got to the door, she stopped before she crossed the threshold; she turned around, and waved into the empty room and said, "Bye Fannie. I'll come back later to play."

Chapter Sixteen

By 5:00 all the small things had been moved into the house. All that was left was the furniture, lawn tools, and the lawnmower. The movers were tired and it was dinner time. The movers left the moving trailer and locked it up for the night and headed into town for dinner and some rest. Eddie locked up the house and they all headed back to the motel. Eddie told Karen about dinner at the Phoenix on their way back. She seemed a little apprehensive but said she would give it a try.

The Phoenix

When they pulled into the Phoenix parking lot, they spotted a prime spot right next to an Impala with a gold star on the door with Morgan County Sheriff's Department written on the fender.

"I guess Alex is already here. You ready?"

Karen checked her makeup in the mirror. "Sure. Let's eat."

As Eddie and the girls stepped through the door, Alex stood up from a table in the middle of the room and waved. "Eddie! Over here."

When Eddie and company got to the table, Eddie introduced Alex to Karen and then to Morgan.

Karen shook hands with Alex and exchanged pleasantries. Alex knelt down to Morgan and shook her hand. Morgan hid halfway behind Karen's leg but was polite. Alex fished something out of his shirt pocket and showed it to Morgan.

"Ya know Morgan, I could use a new deputy on my staff. The sheriff said I could pick anyone I wanted to be my partner. How would you like to be my new deputy partner?" Alex reached out with a plastic deputy badge and clipped it to her overalls.

"Thank you Depedee Alex." Morgan said with a smile as she examined the badge with pride.

They all sat down and picked up the laminated menus. April came over with a tray of glasses filled with water. She set the tray down and served everybody.

"This is April." Alex said. "April this is Eddie, Karen, and my new deputy partner Morgan."

April nodded and said, "It's nice to meet y'all." She took a smaller glass over to Morgan. April had made Morgan a special drink. It was cherry Sprite with a

Vengeful Spirits

miniature umbrella with a cherry stuck through it. April knelt down and placed the drink in front of Morgan.

"I made this just for you. You get the special drink just for new deputy partners." Morgan's eyes were bright with wonder at the neato drink she had been served.

With a big smile she said, "Thank you Miss April."

April handed her a red straw and she immediately took a drink.

"Mmmm…. This is good. Can I have more when I'm finished?"

"You'll have to ask your mom."

Morgan looked pleadingly at Karen. Karen looked at April with a smile and then told Morgan, "I guess so, but don't have too much. Even though you're not driving tonight, we don't want you to start a drinking habit."

Morgan smiled, "Okay mommy."

April took their orders and disappeared into the kitchen. Karen started the conversation. She looked at Alex and asked why they called this place the Phoenix. Alex leaned back in his chair and began his story.

"The house y'all are movin' into was originally owned by a man named Josiah Wells. The place where this bar stands is where Mr. Wells' dry good store used to be. His store was burned to the ground durin' the Civil War. Mr. Wells didn't survive the war so the store was never rebuilt. Eventually Mr. Etheridge, the owner, bought the lot and built this here bar. He thought it would be fittin' to name it the Phoenix."

Jay Duckett

Karen accepted the story with a nod. Eddie had a questioning look on his face and decided to speak his mind. "What happened to Mr. Wells? Did he fight in the Civil War?"

Alex cleared his throat, "I can't tell you what happened to Mr. Wells, but I know he didn't fight in the war. He used his plantation as a restin' point for Confederate soldiers on their way to the front lines to fight. So I don't think he was a soldier."

April came back to the table with drinks. She asked, "Mind if I join y'all?" It was a Sunday night so they were practically the only ones in the building. April could afford to not baby sit the bar for a while.

"No not at all," answered Eddie.

Alex looked at April. "Eddie was askin' about what happened to Josiah Wells." Both April and Alex had grave looks on their faces as they looked at each other.

"What?" Eddie asked.

April held up her hand and looked toward Morgan. "That's a story we'll be savin' for later."

Over dinner Eddie asked Alex, "Do strange things happen on a regular basis around here?"

Alex stopped chewing his food and swallowed then looked sideways toward Eddie.

"Whataya mean….. strange things?"

Eddie told them about being pushed while on the Widow's Walk at his new home. Both Alex and April began to get jumpy and nervous as they listened. Next he told them about the pocket watch and the money. When Eddie finished, Alex had a worried look on his face.

"Do you still have the pocket watch with you?"

"It's at the house still in the box as far as I know. Why?"

"Well…. I was thinkin' maybe April….."

"No!" snapped April. "Not tonight. Maybe some other time."

Eddie and Karen looked at each other in confusion.

"What? What are y'all not saying?" asked Karen.

Alex rubbed his hand over his five o'clock shadow. "Is there anything inscribed on the watch?"

Eddie looked up. "Yeah, as a matter of fact, there is. It says *To my loving husband, Miriam.*"

Now both Alex and April had an ash tint to their faces. Eddie leaned over his empty plate and said, "What the hell's going on here?"

Alex stood up and started walking toward the front wall of the bar. "Come over here. I wanna show you this."

Eddie and Karen stood up and followed Alex. April stood up also, but went over to sit next to Morgan, who was just finishing her bowl of ice cream she had for dessert.

"You wanna 'nother deputy special?"

Morgan looked up and said, "Yeah! That'd be swell Miss April."

April stood up and held out her hand. "You can come with me while I make it. We'll make ya a small one. We don't wantcha gettin' drunk your first official night as a deputy. Do we?"

"Nah, I guess not."

April took Morgan's hand and led her behind the bar where she sat Morgan on the bar while she fixed another deputy special for the cutest little girl she'd ever seen.

Alex stood in front of a picture hanging on the wall just to the left of the door. He pointed to the man in the picture. He was standing in front of a dry goods store. He wore dark pants, a white shirt with suspenders, and had a neatly trimmed beard.

"This is Josiah Wells. The man that owned the dry goods store that used to stand where this bar now stands. He also owned y'all's house during the Civil War." Alex was silent a moment while Eddie and Karen looked closer at the picture.

Karen leaned back, "Who is that standing next to him?"

Alex waited until both of them were looking at him. "That's his wife….. Miriam Wells."

Eddie stood gazing at the image of Josiah and Miriam Wells speechless. If he had questions before, he now had more. He finally found his voice, "The pocket watch! It was Josiah's. Miriam must have given it to him." Eddie thought deeply then thought aloud, "Why do I have it? Where did it come from? And what am I supposed to do with it?"

Karen took Eddie's arm. "Baby, are you okay? You look pale. Come on, let's go sit down." Alex followed Karen as she helped Eddie back to the table. Morgan and April were still at the bar. April was showing her all the neat stuff she used to make drinks. When April saw Eddie walking back over to the table with the help of Karen, she immediately started making a gin and tonic for him to settle his nerves. By the time Eddie was seated, April and Morgan came over to the table and April set the drink in front of him.

"Here. You look like you could use one of these."

Eddie looked at the glass then at April. "How did you know I drink gin and tonic?"

April smiled nervously, "Lucky guess, I s'pose," as she shrugged her shoulders.

As Eddie sipped his drink and the color began to return to his face, Alex asked, "Whataya know 'bout your grandpa?"

Eddie had a questioning look on his face, "Not much really. I think I remember dad mentioning his name was…..Terry…..Thomas….Teddy? Something like that. I remember seeing a picture of him when I was a kid. I think he was in the Army or something. I remember he was wearing a uniform. I remember dad telling stories of winters in Illinois. How cold it was. So I guess he was from up north. If he was from up there then he would have been in the Union Army if my guess at the years are correct." As Alex and the others listened to Eddie dig through his foggy memory, Alex and April looked back and forth at each other with apprehension.

"Why are you asking about my grandfather? Does my grandfather have anything to do with the pocket watch I have?" Then like he'd been hit by a bolt of lighting, Eddie sat up straight in his chair. His sudden movement startled everyone and sent glasses and plates clanging on the table.

"Holy shit!" He looked at Alex with his eyes bugged out and excitement in his voice.

"Do you know what this means?"

Alex nodded his head in understanding. Karen who was sitting beside Eddie asked,

"What? What does it mean?"

Eddie turned. His eyes were afire with excitement. "This means that its very possible that my grandfather was here, in this very town and somehow he knew the Wells. I have some sort of connection to this town and the Wells couple. Eddie finally sat in speechless awe then he lifted his head and said, "This is starting to get creepy."

It was getting late and everybody was tired. After some light conversation about the town to settle everyone's nerves, Eddie and the girls excused themselves. Morgan ran over to April and gave her a hug.

"Thanks Miss April. You make a really good depedee's special." April smiled as she hugged the sweet little girl around the neck. Before Morgan walked away, she whispered to April, "You'll have to come by my new house and meet my new friend, Fannie. Ain't that a funny name?"

April suppressed the jolt of fear that shot through her gut. She put on a big smile and said, "I'd love to sweetie."

Morgan smiled then turned to Alex. She stood straight as a pole and saluted. "Night partner."

Alex saluted back, "G'night deputy partner."

Giggling, Morgan ran to catch up with her parents who were waiting at the door. Eddie made a conscious effort not to look at the picture as he stood waiting for Morgan. Once Morgan joined them, they smiled and said good night to Alex and April who were still sitting at the table.

April sighed and looked at the messy table. "I could come in early tomorrow and clean this up, but I need somethin' to calm my nerves."

Alex nodded his head. "I know whatcha mean. I'll help ya clean up if that's alright."

April smiled. "Always the civil servant, huh?"

As Alex started grabbing plates and glasses, he responded, "That's me. Mr. Civil Servant." Alex paused a moment and watched April then added, "Actually, I wasn't ready to leave you yet."

Alex and April cleaned up the dinner dishes and closed down the bar. Alex stood behind April as she locked the front door. When she turned around, Alex wrapped his arms around her waist and gave her a long passionate kiss. Alex pulled back and looked her in the eyes. "I'm in the mood for some nocturnal activities. How 'bout you?"

April smiled and blushed as she returned his stare. "I was hopin' you weren't outta energy yet. Let's go back to my place."

"Okay. I'll follow ya. See ya there." With a quick kiss, Alex trotted to his car.

63 South Main Street

Once they both were back at April's place and the doors were closed and locked, the clothes came off. This wasn't the first time they had ever made love, but it seemed like it to Alex. They made love on every horizontal surface in the house and even some that weren't horizontal. Eventually they made their way to the bedroom where their lovemaking ended. Both lovers laid on their backs cooling off and relaxing while smoking a cigarette. April finished her cigarette and crushed it out in the ashtray that sat on Alex's stomach. She rolled over and threw her leg over his and kissed his ear.

"I love you baby. You know just how to touch me and make it feel like magic."

In the dark, Alex smiled to himself for a job well done. He was satisfied, she was satisfied, and he enjoyed his cigarette and the sex. What else could he possibly want? He rolled over and quickly fell asleep.

Chapter Seventeen

Madison Manor Hotel

That night, even though he had a million questions banging around in his head, Eddie slept like a log. Knowing he would be able to answer those questions made sleep easier. As he drifted off to sleep, the question of the pocket watch continued to haunt him. *How had my grandfather gotten something so personal that belonged to Josiah?*

At the Wells plantation, two figures sat in the rocking chairs on the front porch. Both figures rocked back and forth enjoying the quiet of the evening. The figure of Josiah now held a gold pocket watch in his ghostly hand, stroking it lovingly with his thumb.

Wells Plantation

The next morning, the moving continued. As the movers moved furniture into the house with Karen's direction, Eddie looked through the other boxes that had been hidden in the attic of the old house. His desk had been brought up to Josiah's old office and placed in front of the window. He sat at his desk and began unloading the boxes. He opened the first box and inside was his father's Klan robe and hood. Under the Klan garb were papers and a photo album. He grabbed the album and began to examine the yellowed memories that his dad had kept. In the front of the album, there were pictures of Klan rallies, cross lightings, and a few lynchings. Eddie pulled the lynching picture from the book and looked at the back. It read *Lynching of Will Clinton, convicted by the Empire of raping a white woman. Justice served July 14, 1918. Polaski, Tennessee.*

He turned the picture over and saw hooded figures holding torches standing around and behind a dead black man's lifeless body. The body hung like a limp dishrag. The front of his trousers were wet at the crotch and his shirt was torn and spotted with blood. His chest had deep cuts and was shining with blood. As he stared at the historic moment caught in time, he remembered the savage beating he had given Alan. With a smile, he flexed his fist. He returned the picture to the book and looked on.

He finally found the picture he was looking for about halfway through the book. It was a picture of a man in a Union army uniform. It was the picture he remembered seeing as a young boy. He removed the picture and closed the book. He sat back in his chair and stared at the image of his grandfather staring back at him. From the look in his eyes, he appeared to be a ruthless, cold man. As he held the picture, images started flashing through his mind. At first the images were of men riding horses and fighting battles in the Civil War then they changed to only six men riding horses. The images continued to change and the speed of the changes sped up. He sees houses burning and women bleeding and crying, clutching their children. He sees men being executed while others stood by laughing. Then he sees Miriam on the floor with a bloody nose and something stuffed in her mouth. He sees black women being pushed by a man holding a rifle. The image of this house flashes in his mind. He sees the front of the house with dead men on the front steps, and a man hanging from the Widow's Walk from a noose. There's another rope there, but no body is hanging from it. Underneath the rope, he sees a lump that looks like a body. Suddenly the visions disappear and Eddie opens his eyes. He looks at the picture in his hand and it bursts into flames. Eddie drops the flaming piece of history to the floor and watches stunned as the picture changes to nothing but ash.

Madison Historical Society

Alex walked into the historical society at ten o'clock sharp. Mark was just hanging up the phone. He looked up.

"Hey Alex. I just got off the phone with the archives. Here's the list of slaves you wanted that were owned by Josiah Wells. Apparently he did have some female slaves. Eight to be exact. Their ages range from fifteen to forty-eight years old."

"Okay. So what happen'd to them? The report didn't mention any female slaves."

Mark shrugged his shoulders. "Maybe they escaped in all the confusion."

Alex scratched his chin as he read the names on the sheet Mark had given him. "No....my gut tells me they never left the property."

Wells Plantation

The afternoon sky had turned cloudy and windy. Eddie sat in his chair looking at the ashes that used to be the picture of his grandfather. *What the hell's going on here?* He reached for the cigar box on the desk. He figured he would check on the other item that had captured his curiosity. As he opened the lid to the box his heart stopped. *The watch is gone again.*

Eddie stood up and started shuffling through the clutter on his desk looking for the watch. "Shit. Where is it? It was here last night."

Eddie thought he heard someone coming up the stairs. He stopped his searching and listened. If it was someone coming up the stairs they were definitely taking their time. Eddie looked out the door in time to see a man slowly walk by the door.

"Hey! Can I help you?" Right away he could tell it wasn't any of the movers. The clothes were different

Vengeful Spirits

besides the man looked too old. He only saw the man from the back so he went out into the hall to find out who it was.

When Eddie got out to the hall, the man was gone as well as the footsteps he heard. The door to the next room over was open. "Ah ha!" As he opened the door and flipped the light switch, he saw an empty room. He was about to turn and leave when he noticed something on the floor under the window. He took a step closer into the room and realized it was the pocket watch. Quickly Eddie took the few steps across the room and knelt to pick up the watch. He held the watch in his hand and put it to his ear. *It's still ticking.* Eddie opened the face of the watch. *The second hand is back and the glass is no longer broken. How did that happen?* As he turned to leave the room, the door slammed shut. It slammed so hard that the frame cracked and splintered. Immediately Eddie reached the door and grabbed the knob. "Ow, that's hot!" He looked down at the knob he had just grabbed. It glowed red. He could feel the heat and smell the wood around the knob as it began to smolder. From behind him he heard a man's voice. Quickly his gut wrenched into a knot of fear. He spun around to see who it was.

Chapter Eighteen

Alex sat in his patrol car staring at the names on the paper that was in his hand.

"C'mon, talk to me." He spoke aloud hoping the paper would talk back. He sat quietly hoping for a revelation or vision, but nothing happened. Alex sighed. "Damn."

Wells Plantation

The movers were all but finished unpacking the moving truck. Only small tables and chairs remained. Once Karen had instructed the movers where to put everything, she looked around for Morgan.

"Morgan?" *She was here just a minute ago.* "Morgan!" Karen quickly walked through the house calling her name. At last she came to the back door. Through the window of the door she saw Morgan standing out in the back yard. Karen opened the door and trotted out to her. When she got to her daughter, it sounded like she was talking to someone. "Morgan. I've been looking all over the house for you. What are you doing out here?"

Morgan turned around at her mother's voice, "Moooomm! You scared away Miss Fannie."

"Who's Miss Fannie?" Karen asked as she looked around the yard for the person Morgan had been talking to.

"Don't you remember? Miss Fannie is my new friend. She was telling me about the people buried here."

A cold chill crawled down Karen's back and the hairs on the back of her neck stood up. "What people? Where?" Morgan pointed at the ground in front of her. When Karen followed the little pointing finger, she noticed several sunken spots in the grass. "There's nobody buried here."

Karen tried to hide her nervousness as she took Morgan's hand.

"Come on inside sweetie."

As Karen and Morgan headed for the back door, Morgan asked, "Do we have a cellar?"

Eddie's knees suddenly turned to jelly as he turned around to see who had spoken. The man standing in front of the window was without a doubt Josiah Wells. His eyes were stern and his expression was nothing short of fury. The man spoke, but his mouth didn't

Vengeful Spirits

move. "Murderer!" The man took one step toward Eddie and the room got bitterly cold. Eddie could see the steady cloud of steam that his breath left. He reached blindly behind him for the door knob. His hand touched the door, but where the knob had been seconds before was now nothing but smooth wood. He looked behind him to confirm what his hands had told him. When he looked back at Josiah, he was standing right in front of him. Josiah spoke again without moving his mouth. "You stole from me once. It won't happen again."

Though the room was as cold as a meat locker, the watch in Eddie's hand began to get hot. Josiah grabbed Eddie's wrist and brought his hand up to eye level. By now Eddie's skin was beginning to melt. No matter how hard he tried he couldn't open his hand. Eddie began to yell in pain and terror. His hand was smoking and he could smell his flesh cooking. Josiah reached up and opened his hand. The flesh peeled away from his hand as his fingers were extended. Josiah grabbed the pocket watch from his hand and put it in his vest pocket. Josiah smiled a wicked smile and said, "Thank you Mr. Stringer. I'm happy to have my property back." As Josiah let go of Eddie's wrist, Eddie collapsed in a heap on the floor.

Karen, Morgan, and the movers were standing over Eddie when he came to.
"Eddie, baby, are you okay? We heard you yelling after the door slammed. We tried to open the door, but it wouldn't budge. What happened?"

Eddie couldn't tell them the truth. Karen loved this house, the financing was a nightmare, and he didn't want to scare Morgan. Besides, the movers would think he was nuts. "I guess a gust of wind blowing through the house made the door slam. I yelled because it scared the hell out of me."

Eddie stood up and avoided eye contact with Karen in the hope she wouldn't notice his lie. "I'm okay baby, thanks."

"You sure you're okay Mr. Stringer," the mover asked.

Eddie nodded his head, "Yeah, I'm fine. Thanks."

Neither Karen nor the movers looked very convinced, but they all returned downstairs except for Morgan, who stood in front of her daddy. She looked up at Eddie with concern in her eyes.

"Miss Fannie says the Master ain't happy." Without saying another word, she turned and skipped down the stairs.

Eddie stood trying to comprehend what happened. As if looking for confirmation, he looked at his left hand. He was afraid he would see a messy glob of melted flesh that was left of his palm. Instead he saw the burned impression of a pocket watch.

Alex decided that since he was getting no where with the names he would drive over to Eddie's new house and see how the moving was coming along. He folded the paper and put it in his shirt pocket. He started the car and headed out of town on Highway 83.

Vengeful Spirits

As Alex pulled up to the house he saw Eddie sitting on the front porch in a rocking chair. The movers were closing the doors on their truck and getting ready to leave. Alex got out of his car and headed for the front porch.

"Hey Eddie." The closer Alex got to Eddie the worse he looked. "You okay? You don't look so good." Eddie made an attempt at a smile. It must not have been much of a smile because Alex asked, "What's wrong?"

Eddie looked at Alex in the eyes and said, "I'm going to tell you something, but don't think I'm crazy." Alex only stared back and shrugged his shoulders.

Eddie told Alex what had happened in the upstairs bedroom then showed him his left hand. When he finished Alex was speechless a moment then found his voice.

"Where's the watch now?"

"I don't know and I don't care."

Just then Morgan came out on the porch and stood in front of Alex. "Hey Depedee Alex!"

"Hey lil' Miss Deputy partner."

"I've got a new friend."

"Really? What's your friend's name?" Alex was trying to remember if any kids lived out this way. He drew a blank. He assumed her new friend was imaginary.

"Her name is Miss Fannie."

The smile disappeared from Alex's face and that icy cold knot in his stomach just tightened. The hair on the back of his neck stood up and he felt the color drain from his face.

Just then Karen stuck her head out the front door. "Morgan honey, let your daddy and his friend talk. Hey Alex." Karen waved and Alex tipped his hat. "Go on inside. I'll be right there." Karen walked over and crouched down next to Eddie. "Do we have a cellar of any kind?" Eddie thought a moment.

"I don't think so. Houses this old don't have basements. The closest thing they had were root cellars. The real estate agent didn't mention anything about one. Why?"

"Morgan keeps telling me Miss Fannie wants out of the cellar. She says she's stuck in there." Eddie had a confused look on his face.

"I haven't seen one, but I'll look. Okay?"

"Okay thanks. You alright Alex? You look a little pale."

Alex nodded his head. "Yeah. I think I'm gettin' a cold though."

"Hope you start feeling better."

"Thanks."

Karen turned and went inside. Eddie turned to Alex.

"What?"

"I know who Miss Fannie is."

"What!?"

"Yeah. Mark down at the historical society got this information from the Georgia Archives this mornin'." Alex unfolded the paper and handed it to Eddie. Eddie looked over names he'd never heard of before. At the bottom of the list was the name of Fannie Mae Stephens.

Vengeful Spirits

Eddie looked up at Alex. "What does this mean?"

Alex looked back at Eddie with serious eyes. "Whatta ya know 'bout the history of this house?"

"Not a whole lot I guess. Why?"

Alex took the rocker next to Eddie and leaned back.

"'Cause there are a few things you oughtta know."

Alex told Eddie the history of the house as best he knew. As he ended his tale

Alex tapped the sheet of paper in Eddie's hand. "These female slaves were not found among the dead. Your daughter's new friend says her name is Fannie, and she's stuck in the cellar." Eddie looked at Alex.

"Let's find that cellar."

Chapter Nineteen

Both men started looking around the foundation of the house. They didn't find anything on either side of the house, but when they got to the rear of the house they found a pair of steel doors hidden behind some overgrown bushes. Alex said with excitement, "This must be it!"

Eddie and Alex pushed through the thicket of bushes that had grown up around the doors. Both of them stood staring at the crudely painted doors. The paint had mostly chipped off and only rusted, bare steel was showing. "Well let's open it up," said Eddie.

The two of them grabbed the handles and pulled. It didn't budge. They continued working at it for twenty minutes to no avail. When finally they decided to rest they sat on the doors panting and sweating. Morgan was watching through a gap in the bushes. Eddie heard her say, "Okay." Then she called out to him, "Hey daddy!"

"Yeah punkin'?"

"Miss Fannie said you'll have to find something to cut the hinges off with. They're rusted shut."

Eddie and Alex looked at each other then got up and stepped out of the bushes. Eddie knelt in front of Morgan.

"Where's Miss Fannie now?"

Morgan hiked her thumb over her shoulder. "She's right behind me."

Eddie looked behind her to see if he could see anything. "I don't see her honey."

Morgan took Eddie's hand and held it over her shoulder. "See? She's right there."

Eddie felt the tips of his fingers start to tingle and get cold. He closed his eyes a moment. He saw a black woman being raped by a young soldier. He was laughing and hitting her. Next he saw a man lying dead in the moonlit grass. The last thing he saw was from the inside of the root cellar, the doors being slammed shut. The sounds of women crying and screaming filled his head. With the bang of the steel doors being slammed shut, Eddie came out of his vision. He opened his eyes and found Morgan smiling at him.

"See daddy she's in there." Morgan was pointing at the steel doors. "Miss Fannie says if you give her a place to sleep all will be forgiven."

The two men looked at each other. Alex had a questioning look on his face.

"So? What did you see? What happened?" Eddie just stared at Alex. He stood up and put a hand on Alex's shoulder and said, "We gotta get those doors open."

Karen was in the kitchen putting dishes in the cupboards. Morgan had come inside and was watching from the doorway holding her Annie doll. "Sweetie, could you come help me for a minute?" Karen turned to look at Morgan, but Morgan shook her head, her pigtails swinging back and forth. "Why not baby? What's the matter?"

Morgan pointed toward the other end of the kitchen. "I'm scared."

Karen sat the dishes down on the counter and knelt down in front of her.

"Why sweetheart? There's nothing to be afraid of." Karen looked where Morgan was pointing. "There's nothing there. It's just you and me." Morgan looked over Karen's shoulder and shook her head again.

"Uh uhh. The missus is here. She's watching you. Miss Fannie says she's angry. Miss Fannie says I should stay away from her."

Karen felt the hackles on the back of her neck rise as a chill ran down her back and collected in her stomach as a knot of fear. Pushing her fear and nerves aside she took Morgan's hands. "There is no missus. This is our house." At that moment the stack of dishes that Karen had left on the counter, crashed to the floor and sent shattered pieces sliding in all directions. The noise startled both Morgan and Karen. Karen spun around and saw what was left of her dishes lying in pieces on the floor. She turned back to Morgan.

She was looking at Karen in the eyes. "I told you the missus was mad."

Eddie and Alex were walking around the house to the front yard.

"We'll need a cutting torch to cut those hinges off."

"Yeah I know."

"There's a tool rental place at the edge of town on 441. We'll need a truck to carry it back though."

"I think Louis has a truck. Let's stop by there on the way to the tool rental place and see if we can borrow his truck."

Alex looked guilty. "I can't go with you. I'm still on duty."

Eddie felt disappointed. It had been a while since he had a friend to pal around with, but he understood. "Oh yeah. I forgot. What time do you get off duty?"

"Uhhh, six o'clock. But it will almost be dark by then. I don't go on duty 'til six o'clock p.m. tomorrow. I can help you tomorrow mornin'."

Eddie perked up. "Okay. That sounds good. I'll go get the torch and the truck tonight. We'll start on it in the morning. One more thing, do you know how to run a torch?"

Karen stood cursing herself for not stacking the dishes properly. In an instant she had convinced herself

Vengeful Spirits

that is why the dishes had fallen. At least that's what she told herself.

When Eddie stuck his head in the door to tell the girls he was headed to town, he found them picking up pieces of dishes on the floor.

"What happened?"

Quickly Morgan spoke up, "The missus is mad." Eddie looked at Karen.

Karen shook her head and responded, "I didn't stack the dishes right and they fell off the counter."

Morgan stood up, "But Momma….." Karen gave Morgan a look that only mothers can give that said "don't say another word". Morgan closed her mouth and went back to picking up the pieces of porcelain that littered the floor.

"By the way, we found the root cellar. The hinges on the doors are rusted and have to be cut off so I'm going to town to get a torch to open it."

Karen looked up in surprise. "We really do have a cellar? What do you think is in there?"

"I don't know, but Alex and I are going to find out in the morning. You two be okay until I get back?" Karen knelt back down and continued to help Morgan pick up the mess.

"Sure sweetheart. We'll be fine. Just be careful."

Eddie surveyed the kitchen before leaving. "Since it doesn't look like we'll be cooking tonight, how about we eat at the Phoenix again?"

As Karen busied herself with her task, she said, "Yeah alright. That sounds good. Maybe tomorrow night we can eat here. There's a lot to be put away, but I'll see what I can do."

"Okay baby. I'll be back in a little while. I shouldn't be long."

161 South Main Street, Ormand and Associates

Eddie pulled up to Lou's office and noticed a red Chevy pick up parked in the spot that was labeled "Louis Ormand Only". Eddie stepped through the door to see Lou's secretary, Dianne Fink, tapping away on the typewriter. She stopped and looked up.

"Mr. Stringer. How nice to see you. Lou has told me all about you." She stuck out her hand and Eddie shook the strong, but feminine hand offered.

"It's nice to see you too. Is Lou busy?"

Just then Lou opened his office door. "Eddie my good man, how good to see you. How's the house coming along?"

"Good to see you too, Lou. It's coming along pretty good. We still have a lot of unpacking to do, but the beds are up, the towels and clothes are unpacked, so at least we'll be able to sleep there tonight."

"Good. Glad to hear it. When will you be able to start?"

"Next week I hope. Is that okay?"

Lou waved his hand. "Sure. Sure. No problem. Do you need any help?"

Eddie smiled. "Well, I could use a favor."

"Anything, you name it."

"Could we swap cars for a day or so? I've got to go over to the tool rental place and rent a cutting torch."

"A cutting torch? What the hell for? Do you even know how to use a torch?"

Eddie tried to hide the flush of embarrassment that burned his face. "Well…..no. But Alex said he thinks he knows how. Besides how hard could it be? I need it to cut the doors off of the old root cellar. The hinges are rusted shut. I.…. I mean we are going to cut the hinges off to get it open."

Lou suppressed a chuckle. "Well since it's a torch you're after, don't go to the rental place. They'll charge you an arm and a leg. Go see my buddy, Jim Caton over at Gaston's Oxygen Supply. He'll rent you the torch and even show you how to use it. On top of that he'll only charge you about half what Chris down at the rental place will charge you. Plus Jim has better equipment. His place is down 441, across from the used car lot. You can't miss it. Tell him I sent you, and he'll take good care of you."

Eddie smiled. "Thanks for the tip Lou."

Lou pulled his keys from his pocket. "Here ya go. It's a three speed on the tree. You can handle that right?"

Eddie gave Lou a sarcastic look and handed him his keys. "It's an automatic. You can handle that right?"

Lou let out a laugh that caused his ample belly to jiggle like a bowl of jello. He slapped Eddie on the back.

"Get the hell outta here."

As Eddie laughed along with Lou, he started toward the door. "Thanks again Lou."

He waved and headed for the Chevy parked at the curb.

Chapter Twenty

Jarrells Estate

Alex finished his shift off by helping Mrs. Jarrells get a fire started in her fireplace. Alex looked in on Mrs. Jarrells from time to time. Her late husband James had been the local Grand Dragon for the Klan in town. He passed away two years ago and left Mable well off. Alex had been knighted into the Klan by James and vowed to James on his deathbed that he would keep an eye on Mable for him after he passed. Mable didn't need much tending though. She was seventy nine years old, but she could take care of herself just fine. Every once in a while she did need help with things that her tired, frail body just couldn't handle anymore. Alex didn't mind though. In fact, he felt it was his duty and an honor to do what he could for her.

With the fire crackling in the fireplace, extra wood in the wood box, and Mable curled up in front of the fire with a cup of tea, he left the house and went to the Phoenix to have a beer and to see April.

Gaston's Oxygen Supply Company

Eddie stepped through the door at Gaston's. He caught Jim filling oxygen cylinders for the local fire department and EMS units. When the bell jingled as Eddie opened the door, Jim looked up.

"Good afternoon. What can I do for ya?"

Eddie looked around the place. It looked like an unorganized hardware store for oxygen supplies. Welding helmets and cutting tips hung from the walls. Gloves, goggles and tip cleaning kits crowded the shelves in the showroom. Eddie could see behind the counter that the rows of shelves in back were as equally cluttered and littered with miscellaneous junk. On the floor all over the place were cylinders of all sizes and types, including different sized fire extinguishers that stood like soldiers on the floor.

"Louis Ormand sent me here. He said you could rent me a cutting torch."

Jim looked Eddie over quickly and noticed his soft hands. "Have you ever used a cutting torch before?"

Eddie reddened as his lack of manly skills was once more brought to light. "No. I've never had the need."

Jim noticed the embarrassment and nervousness of the man, but didn't mention it. Instead, he smiled at

Eddie. "Well...come over to the shop and I'll give you a crash course."

Eddie followed Jim out the side door to the building next door. As he entered the shop, he looked around and noticed that the shop was even more cluttered than the showroom. Of course there were more cylinders, some with caps and valves on them and some were naked. There was a grinding wheel attached to a bench that had bits and pieces of old used metal and broken valves and gauges scattered and stacked on top of each other. Scrap sheet metal, broken gauges, and old metal working tools littered the floor. Some sort of old testing equipment and a winch that hung through the second story floor cluttered the far corner. Tools and junk of all sorts hung from the walls and ceiling. Bare halogen bulbs hung from the ceiling and showered light on the dusty, dirty working areas.

Jim motioned him to come over to the bench in the middle of the room. A hand truck with two cylinders of different sizes sat next to it. Jim stood with a brass tube in his hand. It had hoses coming from one end with two valves at the bottom. The other end looked like a small one sided pick. Jim slowly and carefully explained what everything was and how it worked. When he was finished explaining everything he went over to a pile of scrap and retrieved a piece of metal that he put into the vice. Both men put on their goggles and Jim showed him how to start and set the flame. Jim made the first cut and then let Eddie practice. In less than an hour, Eddie had completed his crash course in torch cutting.

Outside, Jim helped Eddie load the torch set onto the truck and strap it down.

As Eddie left Jim's shop with the torch strapped to the bed, he had pride and confidence in knowing what he was doing.

The Phoenix

Alex parked his car in his regular spot and found his seat at the end of the bar where April had a cold draft waiting for him.

"Hey Baby. How's it goin'?"

Alex finished chugging the first half of his beer. He set the mug on the bar, and said, "I know who owned the platter you touched the other night."

April was suddenly all ears. She leaned on the bar towards Alex and whispered, "Whose was it? Was it stolen?"

Alex finished his beer and quietly set the mug down on the scarred countertop. He looked her directly in the eyes. "It belonged to Miriam Wells."

April had a look of confusion and shock on her face. She got Alex another beer and asked as she set it on the counter, "How'd you get it? And how do ya know?"

Alex had a worried look on his face. He was afraid to tell her the truth as he knew it. "You have to promise me a few things first." April nodded her head quickly. "First, what I tell you stays between us. The story of the truth is ugly."

April nodded, "Okay."

"Second, don't judge me by what I tell you in this story."

April held a bewildered look on her face, but managed to nod her head.

Alex scooted up closer to the bar and leaned toward April. "You know the history of the Wells place, right?"

April nodded her head, "Yeah?"

"Well, my grandfather was one of the men that murdered the Wells back in 1865. His name was James Carter. He was one of two men never caught and hanged for the murders." Alex continued to tell the rest of the story as he knew it. When he finished, April stood staring at Alex with her eyes bugged out and her mouth hanging open. Alex shook her shoulder, "April!"

April closed her mouth and blinked her eyes. "Who else knows about this?"

"No one. Just recently I put all the pieces together and figured it out."

"You have to return that tray."

"To who? Miriam's dead."

"But her spirit is still lookin' for it."

Alex looked at April sarcastically and said, "Yeah right."

"I'm serious Alex." April was grabbing his arm and squeezing it tight. "You came to me 'cause of my talents, right?"

"Yeah?"

"Well my talents tell me that the spirit of Miriam wants her tray back. It must've been special to her."

"Alright, alright. I'll return it to the house. Where should I put it in the house?"

April thought a moment. "Look in the kitchen or dining room for a hutch of some sort. If you find it put the platter on one of the shelves."

"What if I don't find it?"

April put her head in her hands. "If you don't find one, just put it in one of the cupboards in the kitchen, I guess."

Chapter Twenty-One

Wells Plantation

Eddie returns home with the torch, the truck, and an empty stomach. He steps through the door to find Morgan crying and Karen lying on the couch. Morgan rushes up to Eddie and throws her arms around his leg.

"What's wrong punkin'?"

"Mommy told me to shut up about the missus. She said there isn't any missus here. But I saw her daddy. I really did."

"Okay punkin'. Let's go see mommy."

Eddie walked over to Karen lying on the couch. "Hey sweetie. Everything okay?" Eddie sat down on the edge of the couch.

"Yeah, I'm just really worn out, and Morgan won't quit with the missus talk."

"You really upset her."

Morgan peered from behind the wingback chair that sat on the other side of the room. Karen held out her arms.

"Come here sweetie."

Morgan came over and hugged her. Her crying had stopped.

"I'm sorry baby. I'm just not feeling well."

"That's okay mommy. I still love you."

"I love you too, sweetie."

Eddie looked at his watch. "Do you still want to go eat?"

"Nah. My throat's hurting and I don't feel well. Could you bring me something back?"

"Sure baby. You want the same as last time?"

"Yeah. That'll be fine."

Eddie turned to Morgan, "Okay punkin'. Go get your coat."

Morgan ran to the parlor and returned with her coat on and zipped up. "Ready daddy."

Eddie leaned down and kissed Karen on the forehead. "We'll be back in a little while. Will you be okay here by yourself?"

"Yeah, I'll be fine. You two be careful."

Once Eddie and Morgan had left, the house was silent as a tomb. With the blanket pulled up to her chin, Karen quickly drifted off to sleep.

The Phoenix

After Alex and April had decided what to do about the platter, both were silent a moment.

Finally, April asked, "Who was the other man that never got caught?"

Alex looked at her and laughed a tired laugh. "This is where the plot thickens."

April arched her eyebrows. "Really?"

"The other man's name was Thomas Stringer......"

April gasped and covered her mouth with her hand. "You mean Eddie's grandfather?"

"I believe so. I'm convinced that's how he got Josiah's watch. My thinkin' is that after they had killed everybody at the house or locked them in the cellar they looted the place. That's how I ended up with Miriam's platter, and Eddie ended up with Josiah's watch."

April stood shaking her head. "I can't believe this. What are the chances that the two of you would end up in the same town, at the same time, over a hundred years after y'all's grandfathers committed brutal murders?"

Alex smiled sheepishly. "Pretty slim odds, huh?"

Just then Eddie and Morgan came through the door. Eddie waved to April and Alex. Morgan ran over to April, and said, "Hey Miss April, what's a girl gotta do to get a drink in this place?" The three of them looked at each other and laughed. Eddie and Alex shook hands.

Alex looked behind Eddie, "Where's Karen?"

"She stayed at home. She wasn't feeling well so we're going to bring her something back."

April looked over. "I hope she gets to feelin' better."

Jay Duckett

"Thanks. I think she's just worn out from moving. Maybe she just needs to rest a bit."

Alex turned to April. "Can you keep her company for a minute?"

April glanced at Eddie, then back at Alex. "Sure. We'll be over behind the bar."

Alex motioned to Eddie, "Follow me over here for a minute. We need to talk."

Eddie followed Alex over to the far wall with the picture of Josiah and Miriam on it. They both leaned on the wall.

Eddie looked at Alex with concern. "What's going on?"

Alex took a deep breath and let it out. "Remember when I asked you about your grandfather? You told me about a pocket watch and the Confederate money."

Eddie nodded, "Yeah. Why?"

"Well, I think I know how you got the watch. I think you got it from your grandfather. I've also got somethin' that my grandfather had. It has a connection to the Wells too."

Eddie listened intently, then asked, "Well, what's the story?"

"Both of our grandfathers were in the Union army durin' the Civil War. Somewhere along the way, they went A.W.O.L. with six other men. They became known as "bummers". They acted outside the command or orders of the army itself. They did things the way they thought they should be done. I have evidence from historical records that our grandfathers were the only two men who were never caught for the crimes they committed durin' the war. Your grandfather, Thomas, and my grandfather, James, murdered the Wells, their slaves, and looted their home.

Six of the men were caught tryin' to sell the items they had looted. They were tried and hanged for their crimes. For one reason or another, our grandfathers escaped capture, conviction, and hanging. The platter I have and the watch you have both came from the looting of the Wells house."

Eddie's face was pale. He slowly grabbed a chair and sank down into it. He put his head in his hands and took a deep breath. "Are you sure all this is true?"

Alex rubbed his chin and nodded to Eddie. "I've done a lot of research into this. I'm ninety-nine percent sure. From the things you've told me and the things I have dug up, I am convinced that our grandfathers did commit the crimes that are alleged."

Eddie sat up in his chair. "I don't have the watch anymore. I'm not sure where it is now." Eddie reminded Alex of the events that took place on the second floor, first in the office then in the bedroom. "See. Here's the scar on my hand. Remember I told you the story yesterday on the front porch. Since then, I haven't seen the watch anywhere."

Alex looked at Eddie's hand. It had an impression in it that seemed to be molded into the faint shape of a pocket watch in his palm.

"Do you want me to take the platter to the house for you and see what happens?"

Alex shook his head. "Thanks for the offer, but I think I need to return it myself since it was my blood that stole it to begin with. Since it's your house, you don't mind do you?"

Eddie shook his head. "No not at all. Bring it with you tomorrow. When you get to the house just bring it inside with you."

April came walking over with two bags of to go boxes in them. "Here ya go."

Eddie looked at April with surprise. "How did you know what to fix us?"

"Morgan told me."

Morgan stood beside April sipping her depedee special through a straw. She looked up at Eddie and smiled. "Remember daddy? In the car we talked about what we wanted to eat, and remember mommy said she wanted what she got last time."

Eddie smiled at her cute little face, and said, "Oh yeah. I forgot."

Without hesitation, she walked over to the picture of Josiah and Miriam. She pointed at Miriam. "Look daddy. That's the missus that lives at our house."

Alex, April, and Eddie all looked at each other with nervous glances and knots in their stomachs. Eddie looked at Alex.

"You'd better return that platter tomorrow, or someone's going to get hurt for sure."

Chapter Twenty-Two

Wells Plantation

As Eddie and Morgan stepped through the front door at home, Eddie yelled, "Honey, we're home!" There was no answer.

Morgan called, "Mommy! We're back!" Still there was no answer. Both Eddie and Morgan walked down the breezeway toward the living room.

Eddie called out again, "Karen?"

As Eddie looked into the living room, he saw Karen lying on the couch clawing at her throat and kicking violently. Her face was blue and she was gasping for breath. Eddie dropped the food and ran to her side. "Karen! What's wrong?" His mind was blank as to what to do. He grabbed her by the arms and began shaking her and calling out her name.

Morgan stood at the doorway frozen with fear. She found her voice and yelled out, "Don't hurt my mommy!"

Eddie pulled her up by her shoulders to a sitting position. It was then she opened her mouth and took a deep breath. As Karen was gulping air like a fish out of water, she opened her eyes and wrapped her arms around Eddie and began to cry. Eddie held her close a moment until her breathing returned to normal and her crying had stopped. "What happened? Your face was blue and your lips were purple, and my God, look at your neck. It's all red. What the hell happened?"

"I don't know. After you two left, I dozed off. The next thing I remember is not being able to breath. I think I may have had an asthma attack or something. It felt like a sack of concrete was on my chest and someone was trying to strangle me."

Morgan was still standing in the doorway watching. She spoke up and said, "It was the missus. She was sitting on top of you. Her hands were on your neck mommy."

Eddie turned around and looked at Morgan.

"That's enough young lady. I don't want to hear anymore about the missus. There is no missus. Understand? Now I don't want to hear another thing about it. Okay?"

Morgan stuck her bottom lip out and nodded her head. "Okay daddy."

As Eddie turned back to Karen, the logs in the fireplace burst into flame. Karen and Eddie jumped back in shock, and Eddie landed on the floor. They both looked at each other then they looked at Morgan. She looked at them then looked at the fire, smiled and then walked away without saying a word.

After Morgan left, Karen thought about what Morgan had said. Her own words echoed in her mind. *It felt like someone was trying to strangle me.*

The next morning as Eddie was making coffee he heard a knock on the door. He opened the door to see Alex holding a silver serving tray with oven mitts on his hands.
"Hey Alex. What's with the mitts?" Eddie said with a laugh.
"After you told me 'bout the pocket watch thing, I figured that I couldn't be too careful."
"Come on in. I was just making some coffee. Want some?"
"Sure. I'll have a cup."
As Alex walked through the door, he felt the mood of the house change. "Do you have a hutch I can put this in?"
Eddie looked at Alex as if Alex had asked for clam juice in his coffee. "Why?"
"It's a long story. Do you?"

"Yeah. But the doors are still taped up and the hutch is still facing the wall."

"Damn!"

"What? What's wrong?"

"I need a hutch to put this in and it's gettin' hot."

"Are you serious? It's actually getting hot?"

"Yeah. Touch it."

Eddie quickly touched the platter and jerked his hand back. "Ouch! You're right. It is hot." Eddie looked around the kitchen and opened a cabinet door.

"Here put it in the cupboard next to the coffee cups."

Alex quickly dropped the tray on the shelf and pulled the oven mitts off, shaking his hands. "Damn that was really gettin' hot. Look even the mitts are smokin'." Alex put his hand up toward the tray. "You can still feel the heat comin' off it. You think it's safe to leave in there?"

"Sure. I think it'll be alright."

Eddie stuck his hand up to the tray to feel the heat. "What the….."

Alex stepped over. "What? What's the matter?"

"The tray, it's cold."

"What're you talkin' 'bout? It's blazin' hot."

"Not anymore. Put your hand up here."

"Wow. You're right. It sure cooled off fast."

"Yeah. It sure did."

Alex stood staring at the tray. His uneasy feeling was still there. He didn't understand any of this, but hopefully answers were soon to come. Eddie slapped Alex on the back.

"You ready to get at it?"

"Uhh, yeah, I guess so."

Both men went out the back door into the crisp cold morning air. When Eddie reached the yard, he stopped and sniffed the air. "Hey Alex, you smell that?"

Alex was sipping his coffee. "Smell what?" Alex stuck his nose in the air and sniffed. "I don't smell anything."

"It smells like a campfire." Eddie backed up across the yard to get a look at the chimney of the house. "I don't see any smoke coming out of the chimney." Just then his foot bumped something. "Hey Alex?"

"Yeah?"

"Come here a minute."

Alex came walking over. As he got to where Eddie was standing, he looked down.

"Hey looks like you had some hippies spend the night."

Eddie looked down at what was left of the smoldering campfire. "The coals are still warm."

Alex looked out across the pasture and noticed more faint plumes of blue smoke. "Looks like you had a lot of hippies."

Across the pasture Eddie saw a half dozen other dying campfires. All around the fires the grass was trampled, and hoof prints were scattered all over the place. "What the hell's going on here?" A chill ran down Eddie's spine as he looked from the campfires to the Confederate cemetery. Eddie turned to Alex. "Do you think it's possible that…..never mind."

Alex shrugged his shoulders. "Probably just kids or drifters. Let's get started on those doors."

As Eddie and Alex walked back toward the house, Alex looked over his shoulder at the Confederate cemetery and thought to himself, *yeah Eddie I think it just might be possible.* The same chill ran down Alex's back as he remembered what had happened to him in the cemetery only days ago.

Chapter Twenty-Three

Karen was awakened by metallic clanging at the back of the house. At first, she didn't know what the noise was, then she remembered Alex and Eddie were going to get the cellar doors open this morning. She sat up and pulled the covers back. The morning air was cool against her bare legs. She reached up and touched her neck. It was sore to the touch. She thought to herself, *at least I can breathe.*

She went into the bathroom to take a shower. While she was waiting for the water to warm up, she looked at herself in the mirror. "Oh my God!" She saw the scratches on her neck from last nights…….event. Underneath the scratches she saw bruises in the shape of fingers around her neck. The longer she looked she began to see ghostly fingers around her neck. As she stared at the evidence of actually being strangled, a knot of fear and apprehension took hold in her stomach. Finally the mirror started to fog and the hands around her throat disappeared. By now, the small bathroom was full of steam. The shower was ready.

Alex and Eddie had gotten two of the four door hinges cut off, but the door still wouldn't budge. They tried pry bars and hammers to no avail. "I guess we'll have to cut the other hinges off and take both doors off at the same time," noted Alex.

"Yeah looks like it." Eddie fired the torch back up and started on the other hinges.

After Karen's shower, she got dressed and stopped by Morgan's room on her way downstairs. She was just putting her shirt on. "Hey sweetie. You want some hot chocolate with your breakfast?"

Morgan pulled her ponytail out of the collar of her shirt. "Sure mommy." Morgan followed Karen down the stairs to the kitchen.

Karen stuck her head out the back door. She yelled over the noise of the torch. "Eddie!" Eddie stopped cutting and both men looked up. Karen laughed and covered her mouth. With both men looking at her with their welding goggles on, they looked like a couple of giant yard bugs.

Eddie pulled his goggles off. "Hey baby."

"Mornin' Karen."

"Hey you two. While y'all are back here making noise, I'm going out on the front porch to drink my coffee."

"Okay babe."

Eddie and Alex got back to work. Karen watched a moment as they slid their goggles back on and worked on getting the doors open. They reminded her of two little kids playing.

Karen pulled a cup from the cupboard and noticed the serving tray. She poured her coffee and took out the tray. Morgan stood watching the tea kettle warm up on the stove. Karen picked up the tray and looked at Morgan. "Morgan? Where did daddy find this?"

Without looking Morgan said, "It's the missus."

With a sigh, Karen said, "Remember what your father said about the missus?"

Defeated Morgan replied, "Yeah. I remember. But you asked."

Karen grabbed her coffee and the tray. "I'm going out on the front porch. When you fix your chocolate, come on outside."

Morgan was pouting so she didn't answer.

As Karen closed the front door, the tray began to get hot. She dropped it to the floor in shock. She looked at her hand trying to understand what had just happened. As she was looking at her hand, a pressure began to build in her head. At first, she thought that it was a headache coming on, but the pressure continued to build. She closed her eyes against the morning sun thinking that was part of the problem. It didn't help. The pain was beginning to make her nauseous. That's when the crunching noise started. She could feel the noise inside her skull. It sounded like potato chips crunching under foot. She dropped her coffee cup and grabbed her head in an attempt to stop the painful pressure. Just then her nose began to bleed, and her eyeballs felt like they were going to pop out of her skull. She tried to scream, but she felt like she had a mouthful of cotton and her throat was parched. The world began to spin and dizziness began to overtake her. If the painful pressure in her head wasn't enough, her neck began to feel as if it were being stretched beyond its limits. She could feel the tendons and ligaments in her neck begin to pop and the skin at the base of her neck began to tear. The last sound she heard was the sound of snapping bones and tearing flesh as her head was torn from her body.

Her now headless body slumped to the floor in a lifeless heap. Blood spilled from the stump where her head had once been and pooled on the planks of the porch. Her head rolled off her body, bounced once, and rolled to a stop in front of the rocking chair that sat quietly in the morning sun. The last thing Karen's eyes saw was the peeling paint from the underside of the rocker as they remained open in horror and pain and her mouth open in a silent scream.

Morgan sat on the floor in the middle of Fannie's room clutching her Annie doll and crying. The lights were out, but she wasn't scared of the dark. She was scared because she knew something bad had happened to her momma. After Karen had left the kitchen, Fannie Mae had told Morgan she needed to come to her room with her for a little while. Fannie Mae sat next to her with her arm around her. "It gonna be okay baby. You be safe here wit' me."

Morgan slowed her crying, "But my mommy. Something bad has happened."

"I's know baby. Dere's nuttin' I's cud do 'bout dat. All's I's cud do was keeps you safe. Mista Alex an' yo' pappa is findin' me a place to sleep. They bees back soon. Don't you bees worryin' yoself."

After an hour, the other hinges were cut and the cellar doors were finally pulled off and laid in the yard. As Alex and Eddie dropped the doors on the ground, the inside of the doors could be seen. They both stared in horror as the reality of what they were seeing came to life.

Eddie knelt down to get a closer look. "Oh my God! I don't believe this. These look like fingernail scratches."

Alex knelt down on the other side of the door. "Look at this!" His finger was pointing at what looked like old bloody fingernails and bits of dried flesh. At the same time they both looked at each other then headed for the hole that opened into the cellar. Slowly the two of them shuffled closer to the edge of the black hole. The smell of mold and mildew and damp earth wafted toward them. As they peered over the edge of the steep set of steps descending into the blackness, Eddie screamed and jumped back. "What? What is it?" Alex asked, with a tremble in his voice.

Eddie was beginning to hyperventilate, "There's a skull on the steps." Eddie and Alex got up and looked again.

This time Alex gasped, "Oh Jesus save our souls." A skull laid on the second step facing the door. The lower jaw was still attached and the jaws were wide open in a scream for help that was never heard. Alex touched Eddie's arm, "Do you have a flashlight?"

"Why? You're not planning on going down there are you?"

"Well someone has to."

Eddie sighed and gave Alex a stare of resolve. "Yeah it's on the front seat of the truck." Alex stepped over to the truck and retrieved the flash. On the way back to the house, he noticed that there were a lot of crows around the front of the house.

He shrugged it off and rejoined Eddie. "Ready?"

Eddie stood aside, "After you."

Alex stepped over the skull and headed down the steps. The wood of the steps was rotten and weak. Eddie noticed the skull rock back and forth as Alex tread each step. Eddie watched as Alex had reached the bottom and disappeared into the darkness.

"Hey Eddie you gotta see this!"

Fearfully Eddie took a deep breath, steeled his nerves, and joined Alex on the floor of the cellar. Alex showered the floor with light from the flashlight. At their feet, bones of all kinds and sizes filled their vision. Eddie counted seven skulls on the floor, including the one on the steps made eight total. Apparently all the bones that went with the skulls were all on the floor. They were scattered all over the place. Alex spoke what Eddie was thinking, "The rats must've scattered the bones when they ate the flesh off of 'em."

Eddie's throat was sawdust dry. All he could manage to push past his parched vocal cords was, "Yeah."

"I'm going top side," Alex squawked.

"Alright let's go," agreed Eddie.

The air outside smelled sweet compared to the stuffy stench in the cellar. Eddie breathed deep. "Shouldn't we notify someone?"

Alex shook his head. "Those bones are so old there's no way they could be identified."

"So what do we do?"

"I say we bury 'em."

Eddie blew out a heavy sigh. "Okay, but let's get some lunch first."

Alex smiled, "Sounds good to me. You get started and I'll put the stuff back in the truck."

Chapter Twenty-Four

Eddie stepped into the kitchen. Immediately he noticed a heavyset black woman standing at the sink washing something. He stopped dead in his tracks. "Hey who are you? What're you doing in my house?"

The woman didn't budge or turn around. She continued washing as she answered, "Thank you suh for all yo hard wurk. I's real sorry 'bout dat Miss Karen."

Eddie stood in shock and disbelief. He stuck his head out the back door and called to Alex. "Hey Alex! Come here quick."

Alex came running up. "Yeah what's up?" Alex stepped through the door and stood there looking at Eddie. "What?"

Eddie pointed to the kitchen without looking. "Who is that?"

Alex looked over Eddie's shoulder. "Who is who?"

Eddie spun around and looked back to the kitchen. "She's gone."

"Who's gone?"

"There was a black woman standing right there in front of the sink. She was washing something." Eddie walked over to the sink. "See. The water's still running."

Alex came in the kitchen, looked around, and checked out the breezeway. "I don't see anybody. Did she say anything?"

Dumbfounded, Eddie replied, "Yeah. She said thanks for the hard work and she's sorry about Karen."

"Sorry 'bout Karen? What does that mean?"

Worry was painted across Eddie's face. "I don't know, but I think we need to find Karen."

As both men quickly walked the length of the breezeway heading toward the front door, Eddie said, "She told me she was going out to sit on the front porch and have some coffee. We'll check there first."

Eddie pulled the door open and crossed the threshold. As he stepped out onto the porch, he saw the spilled coffee and the broken mug on the floor. He stopped. Alex ran into him from behind, as he closed the door.

Vengeful Spirits

"What? Why did you stop?"

Eddie bent down to examine the mess on the floor. That's when Alex noticed why there were so many crows around. "Oh my God. Eddie?"

Eddie quickly scanned the porch. His eyes came to rest on the headless body of his wife. "KAREN!" Eddie scrambled over to Karen's body screaming and crying. As Eddie scrambled over to her the crows that had been feasting on her body, scattered and flew off, squawking.

Eddie sat on the floor holding the lifeless shell that had once been his wife. Alex, as if in a daze, ran to his patrol car and called in to the dispatcher. Next, he opened the trunk of his car and took out a blanket. Eddie was still holding Karen's body when Alex returned. He took the blanket and covered Karen's head. The eyes were missing and there were peck marks all over her face from the crows feasting. Alex leaned down and put a hand on Eddie's shoulder.

"I called this in. Help should be here soon." After he spoke the words, they sounded so hollow. *Help? What good would help do? It's too late for help now.*

Eddie nodded his head as sobs racked his body and caused him to shake. Suddenly, Eddie's head snapped up. "Where's Morgan?" Eddie started to get up, but Alex put his hand back on his shoulder.

"Easy. Don't worry 'bout a thing. I'll find her."

As Alex stepped away toward the front door, Eddie yelled, "Don't bring her out here! She doesn't need to see this anymore than I do."

Alex held up a hand. "Don't worry. I'll take care of things. I'll be right back."

Chapter Twenty-Five

63 South Main Street

April was at home making herself some lunch. She stood at the kitchen counter putting together some soup and a sandwich. She hadn't felt herself all morning. A feeling of anticipation topped with nervousness and dread had clouded her emotions for the past few hours. About ten minutes ago, the feelings had shifted to agonizing depression and sorrow. As she stood staring at the bowl of soup and the sandwich, she tried to convince herself that she was hungry. She was brought out of her reverie by loud sirens. She looked out the window in time to see a fire engine, ambulance, and a state police car scream by on the street outside. Without thinking she was out the door and in her car.

As she started down the street, another state police car blew by her. She slammed the gas pedal down to the floor in order to catch up with him. The caravan of vehicles blasted through the town square and turned south on highway 83. April was traveling behind the last car. They were well ahead of her, but she could see them well enough to follow. When she saw the police car slide sideways around the corner and head south on 83 out of town, a heavy sick feeling settled in her stomach. *They're goin' to the Wells place.*

Wells Plantation

"Morgan!?" Alex stuck his head in every doorway, upstairs and down. He still hadn't found her. The sick queasy feeling in his stomach turned up a notch. "Morgan?"

Alex stood at the end of the breezeway at the kitchen door. The house was silent. He could still hear Eddie on the front porch. He was hysterically crying over Karen. Off to his left he could hear more crying. He cut through the back of the kitchen. The crying was louder here. He could also hear someone talking over the crying. In the short hallway at the rear of the kitchen, he saw two doors. One was open and one was closed. The noise sounded like it was coming from the closed one. Alex stood with his hand on the doorknob, listening. It sounded like a woman with a thick southern accent talking while the crying continued.

Alex turned the knob and opened the door. The room was pitch dark. He flipped the light switch, and light flooded the room. Morgan sat in the middle of the room on a crude bed. Beside the bed was a small table with an old oil lamp. A dresser with a bedpan and water pitcher occupied the far wall.

Sitting next to Morgan was an older black woman. She was heavy and had streaks of gray in her hair. She had her arm around Morgan comforting her. Alex stood in the doorway staring at the woman. Morgan looked up at Alex. Her face was wet with tears, and her eyes were bloodshot. She slid off the bed and walked over to him. Alex knelt down on one knee and held out his arms. She wrapped her arms around his neck and continued crying. *This poor little girl has been through so much. My heart just breaks for her.* Alex began to cry with her. As they cried together, the woman came over and smoothed Morgan's hair down.

Once Alex stopped crying, he looked at the woman, and asked, "Who are you?"

The woman smiled and folded her hands in front of her. "I's Fannie Mae. I wurk for Mr. Josiah and da missus." Alex's mind was trying to grasp the implications of what she was saying. As if reading his mind, she continued, "Yes suh, I was one of da ones who gots locked up in da cella. Thanks you fo' all yo hard wurk."

Alex closed his eyes and hugged Morgan again. She had stopped crying but continued to sniffle. When Alex opened his eyes again, the woman was gone. The smell of cooked food and sweat she carried with her still hung in the air, but she was gone.

Alex had heard the sirens stop at the front of the house a few minutes ago. Now April was stepping through the doorway out of breath. "Alex, you two okay?"

Alex looked up, "Yeah we're okay, but she's pretty upset." Alex stood up, "She's been back here the whole time. She hasn't seen a thing. She said Fannie told her to stay in here 'til someone came and got her. Somehow I think she knows somethin' bad has happened. I haven't asked her any questions yet. She just now stopped cryin'."

Morgan came over to April and wrapped her arms around her leg. April bent down and gave her a hug. "Can you stay with her for a little bit? I need to give a statement out front."

April nodded her head. "Sure. I can stay here with my favorite little girl."

As Alex walked out the front door, he noticed the paramedics putting the body of Karen in a body bag. Another medic had retrieved her head and was placing it in the bag right where it belonged, atop her shoulders. The blood had dried to a dark brown on the planks of the floor. A state policemen Alex knew walked up the front steps.

"Hey Alex. Were you here for all this?" Alex looked around. He saw Eddie sitting at the back of the

Vengeful Spirits

ambulance with a blanket over his shoulders, and an oxygen mask strapped to his face.

Alex looked blankly at the officer and with a flat tone of voice, he said, "I was here when we discovered the body. Yeah."

"Are you able to give me a statement?"

Alex continued to stare at the state man. "Kevin. The statement I have to give you, you may find hard to believe."

Kevin pulled out his notepad and pen. "Let's give it a try."

Alex told him the history story and then told of the events of this morning. After a while, Kevin quit writing and just listened. When Alex got finished with his lengthy statement, he asked, "Did any of your guys find a silver serving tray on or near the porch?"

Kevin flipped through his notes then shook his head. "No. Why?"

Alex's heart sank. "She didn't know 'bout the tray."

Kevin looked up from his notepad. "What?"

"She didn't know 'bout the tray. It wasn't supposed to leave the house again. She didn't know. Neither Eddie or me had the chance to tell her."

Kevin was staring at Alex with disbelief on his face. "You mean the tray your….."

Kevin flipped through his notes again….. "grandfather stole from here a hundred years ago?"

"Yeah. That's the one."

Chapter Twenty-Six

Alex sighed and stepped off the porch. He got to the ambulance to hear Eddie protesting the paramedics taking him to the hospital for shock. "Hey! Eddie." Eddie turned around. "It's okay. Go to the hospital and let them check you out. Me and April will stay here with Morgan 'til you get finished. Just give me a call here at the house and I'll come pick you up when you're done. Okay?"

Eddie looked Alex in the eyes. "Okay. I'll go. You'll take care of things for me?"

"Of course. What are friends for?"

"What about Miriam?"

"Don't worry. I've made my peace with her. I think Fannie is okay too."

"Fannie? You saw her? What did she say?"

"I'll tell you all 'bout it when I come pick you up."

"Okay. Thanks a million Alex."

"You bet buddy. Give me a call when you're ready to come home. Okay?"

Eddie laid down on the gurney and put the mask back on his face. Alex closed the doors and banged on the back of the ambulance. The police cars and ambulance drove away as the setting sun painted the sky and clouds pink and orange.

Alex stood in the driveway and watched the caravan drive away. As he turned to go back to the house, he noticed the graves of Mr. and Mrs. Wells. The graves themselves hadn't changed, but the ivy that grew on the fence and the surrounding bushes were greener than he remembered.

He walked over to the fence and peered over. He stared in disbelief at what he saw. At the foot of Miriam's headstone, he saw the silver serving tray. Even in the dim light of dusk the platter shined as if it radiated its own light. On Josiah's headstone he saw the gold pocket watch. It too shined in the cold darkness that was closing in.

Alex stood and continued to stare. He rubbed the stubble on his cheeks. "I hope y'all are at peace now. I'm truly sorry for what happened way back when. I never knew my grandfather, and I'm ashamed at what he did here. I hope y'all no longer hold me responsible for what he did." As he finished speaking, a warm breeze blew against his face. He closed his eyes and enjoyed what he felt was absolution. When he opened his eyes again, the platter and watch were gone.

Alex made his way back to the house. He stopped on the porch and decided he should clean up the dried blood before Eddie came back home. In the dark, the blood looked like two black stains on an otherwise white porch. He headed inside to boil some water to help clean the dried scarlet stains from the floor.

Morgan County Medical Center

At the hospital, Eddie had been sedated. By now he was much calmer and his breathing had returned to normal as well as his heart rate and blood pressure. Louis stood by his bed. Both were listening to a football game on the radio that sat on the bedside table.

During a commercial, Lou asked, "Are you sure there's nothing I can do for you?"

Eddie managed half a smile. "Nah. There's nothing I can think of right now. You coming to see me here was more than I expected. Alex and April are at the house looking after Morgan. Everything is pretty much taken care of, but thanks for asking."

"Do you have a ride home?"

"Alex said he would come get me. I just have to give him a call."

"How about I wait until you're ready and I'll take you."

Eddie thought a moment, "Okay. You sure you don't mind?"

Lou waved his hand at Eddie. "Puft. Are you kidding? I don't mind a bit."

Eddie was quiet a moment. He looked at Lou. "I don't know what Alex told the state police, but I think Miriam killed Karen."

Lou's thoughts locked. He never thought he would hear Eddie admit to something like that. He himself didn't believe in ghosts. Sure, he'd heard the rumors about the house over the years, but he figured they were nothing more than local folklore stories.

"She was killed the same way Miriam was. It was like history replaying itself."

Lou shook his head and looked at Eddie with pity. "You don't really believe any of those stories do you?"

Eddie sat up straight in bed, "Lou, Alex told me personally he read the report that was made in 1865 by a Union soldier. What he described to me was exactly what I saw on my front porch this afternoon."

Lou held up his hands as if to fend off Eddie's tirade of conviction. "Okay. I believe that you believe."

Eddie looked at Lou with hurt in his eyes. "You think I'm nuts, don't you?"

Lou smiled back at him. "No. Not at all. You've seen things and experienced things today that I never have. You have a reason to believe, and I don't. But I don't think you're crazy."

Eddie closed his eyes and rubbed his temples with his fingertips. "Why doesn't that make me feel any better?" Eddie opened his eyes and continued, "What frightens me is what might happen to me or Morgan."

Vengeful Spirits

Lou huffed. "I don't think you've got anything to worry about. What happened was a freak accident. I can't explain it, but I surely don't think it was ghosts. I think you and Morgan are completely safe."

Eddie let out a sigh of exasperation. "Well, you keep telling yourself that Lou, but I'm afraid that Morgan and I are not out of the woods yet."

Lou chuckled and slapped Eddie on the back. "I'm sure everything will work out."

Just then the doctor came in. "Well, Mr. Stringer you're looking much better. All your vital signs are normal and strong. You ready to go home?"

Eddie put on a smile. "Sure am doc." Inside Eddie was thinking to himself, *I'm not so sure doc. I'm not sure how safe home is anymore.*

Chapter Twenty-Seven

Wells Plantation

Alex closed the front door. April and Morgan were on the floor of the front parlor playing Chutes and Ladders. April stood up when Alex arrived at the doorway.

"Hey, you okay?" April wrapped her arms around his neck.

"Yeah I'm alright. I'm goin' to boil some water to clean the porch. It should be clean before I bring Eddie home."

"You need any help?"

"Nah. I'll use the hot water to loosen it up then use the garden hose to wash it away. It shouldn't be too much trouble. But thanks anyway." Alex motioned to Morgan, "You keepin' her comp'ny is enough. Poor girl. I can't imagine what she's goin' through."

April kissed him on the lips. "If you need any help, just let me know."

"Thanks baby, I will."

Alex rummaged through the pots and pans in the cabinets until he found a pot large enough. With the pot sitting on the stove full of water, he watched. He then remembered the saying "a watched pot never boils". He decided to go watch a little t.v. in the living room until the water was ready.

He turned on the t.v. and found the Honeymooners, (bang, zooom). He sat on the couch and removed his back up pistol from its holster and laid it on the couch beside him. He leaned back and put his feet on the coffee table. Within minutes he was asleep. He didn't realize how tired he was until he let his body relax.

On the floor in front of the t.v. the burning body of Gregory suddenly appeared. Gregory stood up and stared at Alex's sleeping body with contempt and rage.

Alex was awakened by the smell of smoke. His eyes snapped open. Standing before him was a large man. Not only was the man tall, but he was on fire. Instead of screaming in pain, the man just stared at Alex with angry eyes that seemed to glow brighter than the fire that surrounded him. With the speed of a snake, Alex snatched his pistol and raised it toward the figure to defend himself. Just as quickly, the man grabbed Alex's arm with a vice like grip. With a scream of horror and agony, Alex's arm burst into flame. He dropped his pistol and ran out the back door.

A heavy fog had crawled its way across the field from the cemetery toward the house. Alex didn't seem to notice as he dove into the grass and started rolling on the ground to put out the fire that had begun to consume his flesh.

Both Morgan and April were frightened by the sudden outburst of screaming from Alex. April stood up and looked at Morgan whose eyes had gotten as big as pancakes.
"Stay here. I'll be right back." Morgan could only nod her head as she was frozen with fear.

April ran down the breezeway toward the kitchen. As she passed the living room, she smelled smoke and the stench of burning flesh. The t.v. was still on, but Alex was gone.
She ran out the back door and down the steps. As she got to the bottom of the steps and stepped into the grass, she noticed the thick fog that hung about head high. Through the fog she could see Alex smoking and rolling on the ground yelling. As she approached him, she saw a figure standing over him holding a shotgun to his head.

Alex stopped rolling and laid on his back. When he opened his eyes he saw, through the fog, the silhouette of a man standing over him. He was holding a shotgun to his head. The man said nothing at first; he just smiled as if he was feeding off of Alex's fear. He pushed the end of the double barrels against his head. Alex began to cry uncontrollably and beg for his life. Off to his right he heard April scream, "No! Alex! No please!"

Still holding the gun at Alex's head he turned toward April and sadly said, "I's sorry miss. The good book sez an eye fo' an eye."

April dropped to her knees and began begging as she cried out loud. "Oh God no! Please no!"

The man turned back to the sobbing and begging form of Alex. The man looked down at Alex and said, "Amends must be made." Alex noticed that along with the man in the fog, he could see Confederate soldiers crowded around and watching. April closed her eyes and continued to plead with the man.

The last thing Alex heard was a click as the hammers dropped on both barrels of the shotgun. April screamed in terror as the thunder from the shotgun shook her insides. She opened her eyes and the man was gone. The fog had dissipated as well. All that was left was Alex's body. He laid prostrate on the dewy grass. Steam could be seen escaping from the top of his head where the rest of his skull used to be.

April had lost all grasp of reality. She felt like she was in a dream world. Things like this didn't really happen. She took a few steps toward Alex, but could

Vengeful Spirits

go no further. She saw the sweep of headlights flood across the yard as a car pulled to a stop in front of the house.

In a daze, April staggered around the house toward the front and met Eddie and Lou as they got out of Eddie's car. Eddie ran over to April. "Hey. You alright? You look terrible. What happened?" April's face was tear-streaked, her makeup was smeared, and her hair was tossed in all different directions. At first glance, she looked like a woman on the edge of insanity. She began babbling and muttering incoherently. All Eddie could make out was that Alex was dead. Eddie sat her down in the passenger seat. "Is Morgan still in the house?" April only nodded her head.

Eddie looked at Lou in the eyes. "Stay here with her. I'm going to get Morgan and I'll be right back." Lou stood beside the car in confusion, but managed to nod and mumble, "Okay."

Eddie took off running toward the house at full sprint. He jumped the porch steps and ran across the porch so fast he didn't even notice the blood stains on the floor.

He burst through the front door yelling Morgan's name. He glanced in the parlor and saw a game on the floor. Its pieces were scattered all over the place. "Morgan?" He continued down the breezeway yelling her name as he looked into each room. "Morgan!" As he passed the living room, he smelled smoke and burned flesh. His gut wrenched at what might have happened to his daughter. "Morgan?" He reached the kitchen and found a pot of boiling water bubbling on the stove. "Where the hell can she be?" He turned from the kitchen and ran to Fannie's room. He kicked open the door and found Morgan sitting on Fannie's bed with Fannie sitting next to her. "Morgan!" Morgan looked up. She was crying uncontrollably. Tears streamed down her face. Her wracking sobs caused her body to slightly convulse. She quickly slid off the bed and ran to him. Eddie knelt as she got to him. "Honey we've got to go. We can't stay here anymore."

Morgan looked up at him. Between sobs she said, "Fannie said I could stay, but you couldn't."

Eddie looked over at Fannie. "Thank you for looking after her, but we must go."

Fannie stood up from the bed. "Wheres you think yous goin' wit her? She da only happiness I's had in ova a hunned years. I's ain't gonna let her go." Her face had gone from pleasant to fierce at the mention of Morgan leaving.

Eddie turned around. "We're leaving." Eddie picked Morgan up and carried her down the breezeway toward the front door. Just before they got to the door, Eddie felt a pull on his arm. It was Fannie. He turned around to face her as he put Morgan down and she hid behind his leg. By now Eddie was scared and angry. "Look! I'm sorry for the things that happened to you in the past, but we're leaving now."

Fannie put her hand around Morgan's arm. "Like hell you is."

Vengeful Spirits

From behind, Eddie heard the gruff voice of a man. "Fannie! Let her go." Eddie spun around. It was Josiah. He was standing between him and the door.

"Let her go Fannie. She's not yours to keep."

"But masta?"

"No buts Fannie. Let her go."

Reluctantly, Fannie released her grip on Morgan. She now had a sad look on her face as she turned and walked back down the breezeway. Before she had gotten to the end of the hallway, she had all but disappeared.

Chapter Twenty-Eight

Eddie turned back to Josiah. "Thank you, sir. I….." Josiah put up his hand to stop Eddie from saying more. He stepped aside and opened the door. Eddie began to walk out the door, but Josiah put his arm across the open doorway.

"Your daughter may go, but you and I have some unsettled business to deal with."

With heavy dread, Eddie knelt down to Morgan, and said, "Go sit with Miss April and Uncle Lou in the car. I'll be right there." He gave her a kiss and she hesitantly shuffled across the front porch where Lou picked her up to take her back to the car.

"I'll be out in a min…."

Josiah slammed the door shut before Eddie could finish. "What's this unfinished business that we have? You got your watch back." Eddie noticed dangling from Josiah's left hand was a noose. Josiah brought the noose up to Eddie's face. Cold fear gripped Eddie with hands like a steel trap.

Josiah smiled. "It's time to pay for your sins."

Eddie began to shake as he saw no way of escape. Sweat poured from every pore in his body. Josiah continued to smile. "The way you're feeling now? That's exactly how I felt when Thomas dragged me up these very steps before he murdered me and my wife."

Eddie worked to make his numb lips and dry throat speak. "Bbbuutt that was my grandfather. Nnnoott me."

"That's too bad. Your grandfather died in his sleep before he could pay the price. Your father died of a heart attack before he could pay. You are my last chance at leveling the scales of justice."

"Oh please, not me." Eddie began to cry.

Josiah began to laugh. "That's funny. I pleaded with your grandfather just the same way. It didn't change things for me either." Josiah began to walk toward the steps. He grabbed Eddie's arm. "Time to go." Eddie pulled free of his grasp and grabbed the doorknob. The sound of frying eggs and burning flesh filled the air as the doorknob began to cook the flesh from his hand. Eddie screamed out in pain as he pulled the smoking hand free of the knob. "I said let's go." A force like nothing he'd ever felt before hurled him from the doorway halfway up the steps.

Vengeful Spirits

Josiah made his way up the steps behind Eddie. "That's the spirit." Eddie could feel the ends of his broken ribs rub together with every breath he took. Pushing down the pain, he scurried up the steps staying ahead of Josiah.

As Josiah reached the landing, Eddie pleaded with Josiah again. "I'm sorry. If I could change the past, I would."

Josiah nodded. "I would too. I would have much preferred to deal with your grandfather personally, but things didn't work out that way. Now keep moving."

Eddie didn't budge. Again, an invisible force grabbed Eddie and threw him all the way down the hallway where he crashed into the front wall of the second floor.

Lou, April, and Morgan sat on the hood of Eddie's car and waited for Eddie to join them. "What is he doing in there?" Lou paced in front of the car. April held Morgan close to her with her coat wrapped around her to keep her warm. Just then the porch lights came on and the doors to the Widow's Walk exploded sending wood and glass raining all over the front yard. Lou and April ducked for cover as glass and pieces of wood pummeled them and the car.

"Good Lord! What the hell was that?" Lou peeked his head out from underneath his coat to see the carnage that littered the yard.

April poked her head out of her jacket and yelled, "Look! Isn't that Eddie? What's he doin' up there?"

Jay Duckett

After the glass doors had exploded, Eddie appeared on the Walk. He had something hanging around his neck. With horror, April realized it was a noose. The figure of Josiah appeared behind him. Eddie was crying and babbling as Josiah tied the end of the noose around the railing. April stood and stared in horror as she realized what was about to happen. Morgan peeked from around April's jacket and looked at her father. April quickly took the jacket and covered her face with it. She knew what was gonna happen, but there was nothing she could do about it. She did the only thing she could do, she spared his daughter from having to see it happen.

Lou's voice startled April. "What is that?" Lou was pointing at the front steps. All along the steps the ghostly figures of slaves watched quietly as historical events took place. "What's going on?" asked Lou.

April said, without looking at him, "Something we can't stop."

Up on the Widow's Walk Josiah leaned over Eddie's shoulder and whispered into his ear, "You're getting off lucky. You're heavy enough, your neck will snap when you reach the bottom. Me, I almost strangled to death before your grandfather gave one last jerk of my legs in order to break my neck and put me out of my misery. As I see it, once this is done, our business is over with, you're free." With that, Josiah shoved Eddie over the railing.

Lou and April both gasped in horror as they watched Eddie topple over the railing and fall. As the rope went tight, Lou and April cringed when Eddie's body snapped down and they heard the pop and crunch as his neck snapped in two.

Back on the Widow's Walk, the figure of Josiah faded away like fog from a mirror, and the porch lights went out. The slaves that had watched from the steps turned and began walking away. The further away they got the quicker they faded into the darkness until they disappeared. Lou looked at April. "What the hell just happened?"

With no expression, April responded, "A hundred years of bottled vengeance released."

Lou looked at the house. "We should get Eddie down."

April grabbed his arm as he started toward the house. "Use the radio in Alex's car and tell the dispatch to get the state police and coroner back out here. They'll want to talk to us when they get here."

"What are we gonna tell them?"

"I don't know about you, but I'm gonna tell 'em the same thing I told 'em 'bout Karen's death."

Lou waited. "Which was?"

"The dead can finally rest. The price has been paid in full. The dead never seem to forget."

Morgan stuck her head out of April's coat and looked up at April. "The ghosts are gone, aren't they?"

April stroked Morgan's hair as she looked down at her. "Yes baby they are."

"Mommy and daddy are gone too, aren't they?"

April began to cry again as she couldn't answer past the sobs instead she held Morgan tightly against her.

Epilogue

The bodies of Alex and Eddie were identified and removed that night. Alex's body was buried in the city cemetery at the south side of town. He was given full law officer honors. His plot sits next to other law officers that had died in the area dating back to 1868.

Both Eddie and Karen were laid to rest underneath an oak tree at the far side of the Confederate cemetery at the request of Lou, who was named the executor of the Stringer estate.

Morgan stayed with April while the paperwork was being completed for April to adopt her. Neither Eddie nor Karen had any family left for Morgan to live with. The state, along with Lou, felt that being with April was the best place for Morgan. Both are seeking counseling for post traumatic stress.

The State District Attorney questioned both April and Lou about the events that had taken place at the Wells plantation. Lou wasn't much help due to the fact that he had been kept in the dark for most of the time. April, however, answered their questions. The District Attorney found it hard to believe or accept the ghost story that April gave as her statement. To this date, the case remains open and unsolved.

The pot that Alex had left on the stove had caused a fire. The fire had consumed the entire house down to the rock foundations. After the fire, the skeletons of the entombed slaves in the root cellar were found. As local historian, Mark Prather, had been called to the scene to document and confirm their identities. The bones were reassembled as much as possible by the county coroner. Then the bones were buried along with the other slaves at the rear of the house.

The city eventually bought the land from the Stringer estate. It is now a city park. There are plaques here and there documenting the story of the land from the time Josiah bought the property to the time the Stringers were murdered.

The life insurance, fire insurance, and sale of the property were put into a trust for Morgan. Morgan will be able to draw from the trust after her twenty-first birthday.

If you ever find yourself in Madison, Georgia you should stop by and visit the "Pasture of Grace". Rumors say that at night you can hear horses running, cannon fire, banjo music, and see a host of friendly ghosts, and if the wind is right you can smell Miriam's stew cooking over a campfire.

About the Author

Jason Duckett is thirty-five years old. He resides in Snellville, Georgia about twenty miles northeast of Atlanta. He is a full time mechanic at an independent repair shop in Atlanta. He is single and has no children. This is his first book. His writing has been inspired by authors such as F. Paul Wilson, Tamara Thorne, and John Saul. If your imagination is captured by these authors this book is sure to please. The house that inspired this book is real. It is located about halfway between Bostwick, Georgia and Madison, Georgia on Highway 83. He is currently working on a second book inspired by a location in central Georgia. He welcomes readers to contact at his email address at: rebelguns@hotmail.com.

Printed in the United States
54859LVS00001B/84